THE CASEY STONE SERIES:

Alias Baby Girl

A Casey Stone, P. I. Mystery

ROBERT W. GODWIN

HILLIARD HARRIS

HILLIARD HARRIS

P.O. Box 84
Boonsboro, Maryland 21713-0084

This novel is a work of fiction. Names, characters, places and incidents either are the product of the author's imagination or are used fictitiously. Any resemblance to actual persons, living or dead, events, or locales is entirely coincidental.

ALIAS BABY GIRL Copyright © 2010-2021
By ROBERT W. GODWIN

First Edition—2010-2020
ISBN 1-59133-466-7
978-1-59133-466-8

Book Design: S. A. Reilly
Cover Illustration © S. A. Reilly
Manufactured/Printed in the United States of America
2010-2021

Acknowledgements

I have found that any book is a collaborative effort and wish to acknowledge the following persons.

Don Williams, columnist, author, publisher of *New Millennium Writings*, and leader of my Creative Writing Class whose personal input and guidance were most valuable.

Members of said Creative Writing Class who contributed their reactions, comments, and encouragement as the book was being written.

Janet Fluri, my beloved secretary for over forty years who suffered through the many rewrites and revisions.

My agent, Janet Benrey, who believed in the book and diligently worked to see it published.

Stephanie A. Reilly at Hilliard & Harris Publishers, who patiently worked with a novice to bring his first novel to the public.

Mickey Spillane died July 17, 2006 at the age of 88 from pancreatic cancer. He introduced his iconic private investigator, Mike Hammer, in the 1947 novel I, The Jury. Spillane called himself a writer, not an author, i.e. someone whose books sell. This is a tip of the fedora to his memory.

CHARACTERS

Casey Stone—New York Private Investigator
Rosemary Kelly—Client trying to locate adopted daughter
Joey Catalano—Minor, but dangerous mobster
Chiquita—Longtime secretary/assistant to Casey Stone
Pat—Owner of Pat's Bar and Grill
David Greenberg—Attorney for the trust fund
Maureen—Receptionist at Greenberg's Law Office
Manny—Owner/operator of a Midtown deli
Steve Butler—Good cop and longtime friend of Casey
Janie Butler—Steve Butler's wife and mother to their six-month-old daughter
Suzie Oh—Clerk in uncle's Chinese laundry who meets and falls for Casey
Sam Napolitano—Longtime mob goon who works for Joey
Felix—The other goon that works for Joey with an unknown past
Simon Rosenthal—CPA for The Home
Joseph K. Menaphy—Wealthy patron and board member of The Home
Judge Hubert McNair—Family law judge who signed the adoption order for Rose's baby
Maria Fregossi—Legal secretary to Judge Hubert McNair
Carl—Casey's auto mechanic, an East Tennessee native
Luther—Superintendent of Casey's apartment building
Jimmy—Runs a newspaper/magazine stand
Queenie—Retired secretary to precinct captain; owns a diner frequented by cops

Chapter 1

"Your door says Casey Stone, PI. Pat, around the corner, said you knew what you were doing and knew how to keep your mouth shut."

I swung my feet off the desk and snubbed out my Camel. Worrying about how I was going to pay my bar tab, I hadn't heard her come in the outer office. Pat owned Pat's Bar and Grill, one of the few real friends I had in Manhattan and the holder of my bar tab.

"I'm Stone. Secretary is on break. Can I help you, ma'am?" Her hair was a little too big, her skirt was a little too short, her heels were a little too high, her blouse was a little too low—and she looked just right to me.

She stepped through my door and walked to the worn wooden chair in front of my desk. Watching her walk across the room was like watching a pillowcase full of kittens. She crossed her legs and deliberately leaned forward, crossing her arms over her legs. It had the desired effect of riveting my attention.

"I have a problem."

"Welcome to the club." I immediately regretted my flip remark. It was stupid for a broke gumshoe down to his last c note to crack wise with a potential client.

"Sorry. I won't take a job unless I can do it and I keep my mouth shut. So, what can I do for you?" I tossed it back to her like a medicine ball at the Downtown Athletic Club.

We sat looking at each other, the silence covering the bare desk between us like a worn tablecloth. I picked up the pack of Camels and tapped one out. I knew she would take it before I offered. I tapped out another for me, and then lit both of us with my Zippo. I took a deep drag and tilted my chair back, blowing a cloud toward the ceiling. Her eyes never left my face.

She was early 30's, I guessed. Her baby blues had seen a lot of life. Her face was still pretty and her blond hair had never heard of peroxide. But there was a hint of sadness underneath the brass and the bold stare. The rest of her was even better than her face.

She knocked the ash off her cigarette, leaned back and crossed her legs the other way. They were long enough to reach New Jersey, and I had a hard time paying attention to what she was saying.

"I had just graduated from high school and was madly in love with a boy I thought I'd marry. As soon as he found out I was pregnant, he dropped me, disappeared from the block and joined the Army. As soon as my folks found out, they gave me an hour to choose between an abortion or getting out of the flat. That's the way it was in 1943.

"I packed a few of my clothes and spent a couple of nights in Grand Central Station before I saw a notice and found my way to The Home. They fed and housed me for the next six months, but the price was signing away the baby as soon as I delivered. She was a beautiful baby girl. I was crying so hard they had to hold the pen in my hand for the signature. Three days later, I was back on the street with nothing but the clothes on my back and a hole in my heart. I cried for weeks, but I could hardly take care of myself, let alone a baby girl. It was the only thing I could do." She took a drag off the smoke like a drowning man coming up for air. Her voice wavered, but there were no tears. Her eyes looked through my office wall at time and events long ago. After a second drag, the eyes came back to me.

"That was sixteen years ago. There hasn't been a day since that I haven't thought of her. I call her Angel. I want you to find her."

It was a story I'd heard before, but I never got used to it. "Look, Miss..."

"Rosemary Kelly. They call me Rose."

"Look, Miss Kelly, she's got her own life now...parents, maybe even brothers and sisters. She's about as old as you were when you had her. She doesn't know you. She may not even want to know you. Why do you want to stir all of that up now?"

"I keep books for a shipping company. It isn't much, but it pays the rent, and the boss keeps his hands to himself. Last week a fancy suit came by asking for me. The girls at the front figured he was a bill collector and told him they'd never heard of me, but he came back the next day, left a card, and said it was extremely urgent.

"The card said he was a lawyer with a big Midtown law firm, not a two-bit shyster chasing an overdue bill. I called. I didn't tell him who I was, except that he'd left his card hunting a 'Rosemary Kelly', and I might know her. He said he didn't exactly want her, he wanted her kid. I almost dropped the phone. 'Her kid?! What for?'" Her smoke had one good drag left, which she took without thinking.

"Turns out the jerk that dumped me had a conscience. He was a helicopter pilot in Korea and went back overseas when he finished his army duty. He fell into something good. Mr. Greenberg...that's the lawyer...couldn't or wouldn't say what it was, except that about eight years ago he retained the firm to set up a trust fund for my baby. He made deposits to the trust every once in a while. Then he died two months ago somewhere in Asia and that triggered the trust.

"Mr. Greenberg said it wasn't hard to find me...East side neighborhoods are pretty stable and all the families on the block know everything anyway. And I get along with my folks now. But I'm the only one that knows anything about my baby, and suddenly she is entitled to more than a million bucks.

"There's a catch, though." There always is, I thought, or they wouldn't come to see me. "They have to find my baby within thirty days or the trust goes to the jerk's worthless

3

younger brother." Her eyes got hard and she snubbed out her smoke with a sharp jab. "Of course, Joey...the slimy creep of a brother...knows he'll get the million if she can't be found or if she's dead. He's been pushing drugs since he was in junior high school and has been in a bunch of rough stuff, but he never did hard time. He's always beat it. He's got connections. He'd off her in a minute. So, it's a race, Mr. Stone. You've got to help me find her."

"You don't know what you're asking, Miss Kelly. I've dealt with those homes before. They'll take in a girl that's got no options and basically steal their baby. It's a racket, but they've got lawyers on the payroll to make sure you can't change your mind. And once there is an adoption, the court seals the records and you can't blast them loose with an atomic bomb."

She wasn't fazed a bit. "Mr. Greenberg said he knew it would be difficult, but the trust was authorized to advance me money for the search to use as I see fit." She reached in her bag, pulled out an envelope and scooted it across the desk to me. "Here's $2,000.00 cash."

"There's really nothing I can do, Miss Kelly." It took all my strength to push the envelope back toward her, but I had never stiffed a client before and wasn't going to start now. She didn't touch it.

"I think you can, Mr. Stone. You see, I was underage when I signed."

Chapter 2

I got details from her on The Home. I got details from her on Joey. The more I heard, the madder I got.

The Home made a mockery of the name; prison would have been more accurate. Their deal was tasteless food and a cell in exchange for the baby. You couldn't even sit on the reception room chair till you had signed away your rights in triplicate. The house matron should have been in a Nazi uniform. They used the girls for chores—hard manual labor—right up to the time their contractions started. A delivery room in the basement was operated by a quack who had his license lifted in Jersey for illegal abortions. After delivery, they pushed you out the door.

Joey, the younger brother, put a move on Rose as soon as she showed back up in the neighborhood after she had her baby. She got a job at Manny's Deli at the end of their block. Joey caught her one night taking the trash out to the dumpster in the alley. After he made a gutter remark and grabbed at her, she hit him with the trashcan. He smashed her head against the dumpster and was ripping off her clothes when Manny came to investigate the racket and ran him off. Joey sent word through some of his pals that she'd pay and pay big. As time went by and he got a tougher reputation, she worried more and more about him. When she got a better job and moved downtown, she had to sneak back onto the block to see her elderly parents.

I could hardly wait to get my hands on him. I hate the bastards that thumb their nose at society and chew up the defenseless. I carry a piece and have a license for it. When I use it, I intend to kill. But I make it legal. Sure, there have been some bleeding hearts that slammed me in the papers: "blatant disregard of rights, loose cannon on the deck, menace to law-abiding citizens." I've even been hauled to court a couple of times on criminal charges, but I beat 'em. I beat 'em because I'm careful to make it legal. The difference between the cops and me is that I don't have twenty layers of bureaucracy, rules, and regulations on top of me. I think fast, I act fast, and I'm still here with my rod. The creeps know how I am, and that's why I usually get the job done.

I got Rose's phone number and address—a tiny walk-up not far from my office—and told her I'd be in touch when I knew anything or had further questions.

I watched her exit the office as Chiquita returned. The women eyed each other like two cats passing on a picket fence.

"So who was that?" My long-time secretary said, icicles hanging off every word.

"It was strictly professional," I replied.

"Yours or hers?" she snapped.

"Hey, lighten up, Toots. She paid your salary and the rent for a couple of months. We've got work to do."

Chiquita was classic Puerto Rican: dark skin, shiny black hair, red lipstick, and standard issue hoop earrings. Yeah, and she had a brother named Jesus. She held a PI license and had a carry permit for her .32 Beretta. She qualified every month at the firing range and kept in shape with twice weekly Judo sessions. And shape she had, but from the day I hired her we had an understanding that there was no office hanky-panky, an understanding I frequently regretted. Even so, every time I had a female client, I got a closer inspection than I ever did in the Army, with explanations demanded for every loose hair or lipstick smudge. I kept her because she was good in the office, good in the field, and good with the clients, at least when she was satisfied I wasn't tumbling into the hay with them.

I briefed her on the case and told her to dig up everything she could on The Home—it was still in the phonebook. She listened intently, took a few notes, and got as mad as I was. "Some of my girlfriends got in trouble and had to go away for a few months. I know about places like this. The stories they would tell me when they came back made me hate the…" Her sentence dissolved in a torrent of Spanish that I couldn't translate, but understood perfectly. She left in a swirl of black hair, fiery curses and stiletto heels. I could hear her all the way to the elevator down the hall. I wouldn't want to be the one who crossed her today. She was only 5'3" and even in her Judo pajamas looked sexier than those runway models. Many a training partner made the mistake of thinking his workout was going to be loaded with extra benefits. The only extras they got were bruises.

I grabbed my hat and jacket, locked the door and went to thank Pat for sending the broad to me. I paid up my tab, put down a healthy advance and had a tall one before I headed uptown. On a whim, I asked Pat if he'd ever heard of Manny's. Pat grinned ear to ear and said, "You tell that big ox he owes me a ten spot for the last Yankees' game, and I want it paid, in person, right here, at my place, by Sunday! And if he gets stormy on you, tell him that I also said the first six beers are on the house."

I caught the subway north and walked the rest of the way east.

Manny's looked just like every other neighborhood deli in the city. The sign and the window lettering were at least twenty-five years old and the window was filled with posters and notices on everything from fights at the Garden to Easter programs at P.S. 231. I pushed through the lunch crowd and took a stool at the counter. I barely had time to scan the blackboard menu before my view was blocked by a 300-pound bald whirlwind in a white apron, black mustache and Friar Tuck fringe. I ordered the daily special—kielbasa with white beans, cornbread, onion slice and a tall glass of ice-cold milk. He yelled the order to two dervishes working the grill, slicer, and steamer, and had my money before I could take a deep breath.

The food was good and came quick, but I ate slowly and scavenged the sports section of the daily paper from beside the cash register. I was into my second cigarette and on the last page of baseball stats when Manny loomed over the counter.

"You aren't from around here. Need anything else mister?" There was more in his words than the simple question.

"Just waiting till the crowd thinned, Manny. I'm told you welshed on a $10.00 bet on the last Yankees/Red Sox game. And I'm here to tell you to deliver it, in person." Red began to flood his face and the two dervishes in the back froze. I figured I'd better get the rest of it out fast or I'd be flatter than a slice of his bologna. "And deliver it in person to Pat's Bar, and he says the first six beers are on him."

The red reached all the way over his head to the back of his fringe. Then the explosion came. Lucky for me it was laughter, a great roar of mirth which rocked me back and restarted the dervishes on their chores with their own chuckles of relief.

He came around the end of the counter and waved me to an empty booth at the rear, which creaked as he squeezed in. "I bet you didn't come all the way up here just for that."

"I'm working for Rose Kelly," and flashed my ID. Manny was big—and fast. He palmed the ID and studied it a lot longer than he had to. I got the point: I was still there on approval.

"So," he said, flipping it back to the table, "are you going to treat Rose right, or are you one of those sleaze balls that rip people off that are already getting screwed?" His voice was like a rusty trombone. He leaned forward as much as his girth would let him, and continued a little bit lower. "That girl was treated like crap by that boy who knocked her up, her folks who kicked her out, that so-called Home, and that little shit Joey who tried to rape her outside my back door. I kicked his ass half way down the alley and told him he was going through my slicer if he ever came around again. And I'll do the same to anybody else who leans on that girl." He was one of the good guys, but he didn't know we were on the same team yet.

I told him the deal and my plan to pay a little visit to Joey, just to let him look at somebody who didn't care if he was a junior wise guy, and disabuse him of the idea that he needed to be looking for the kid. By the time I finished, I was looking at an enraged grizzly bear. I had to calm him down some or he'd screw up the whole thing.

"Look Manny, this is my gig. I'm getting paid to be the point man, but I need help. Don't stick your neck out and get your ass shot or your place torched. What I need is your eyes and ears. I saw who was coming in here. Your regulars know everything on the street. Find out what you can on who's got connections with The Home; particularly anybody who's been there a long time and knows their MO. I need to crack that confidentiality wall and start tracing that kid. The trail is sixteen years cold and there isn't much time. First thing, though, just tell me where I can find Joey."

The bear growled. "I should have killed the bastard when I had the chance." He simmered a while before continuing. "OK, shamus. Joey works out of a backroom at Chen's Laundry four blocks up east of here. He's got his fingers in a little bit of everything: drugs, numbers, a few girls, and protection in about a twelve-block area. He's not a big fish, but he's got enough influence at the precinct to avoid trouble most of the time, and enough mob connections to help out at the courthouse when he does step in something. Be careful, Stone, this isn't your part of town. You step lightly."

At 6'2", 190 pounds, I might have looked wimpy to this bear, but I've never stepped lightly in my life. That explains the dents in my skull and the scars here and there that have made for some interesting conversations with sympathetic ladies.

"Thanks, Manny. Don't worry about me. I've been around the block a couple of times." I let my coat sag open to show a bit of my holster. He saw enough to know it was a .45 automatic.   I gave him a card and he promised to call me with any scoop.

We were friends now.   He even gave me a pat on the back on the way out.   I figured I'd only be sore a couple of days.

Chapter 3

The weather was too nice to take a cab, so I decided to walk the few blocks up to Chen's. I came to a phone booth and dropped in a nickel. I dialed the office and wasn't surprised when there was no answer. I knew Chiquita was going to hit several offices, and this time no news was good news.
I broke connection, dialed the Downtown Precinct and asked for Captain Butler. The desk sergeant said he was on another phone and to hold the line.

Steve Butler was a good cop—most of them were. They were overworked, overloaded with paperwork, under-appreciated, and underpaid. Just to make it all come out right, they got to put their lives on the line, over and over.

Steve and I didn't start out as bosom buddies. We met on a murder case several years ago when the victim's family wasn't sure the police were really working the case. The family hired me, and I made a courtesy call to the precinct. Steve was just a sergeant then and resented the implication that he couldn't or wouldn't handle the job right. I thought he was pig-headed and told him so. He told me I was sticking my nose where it didn't belong, and it just might get busted. By the end of the case, we'd helped each other solve it and become pals in the process. It didn't hurt that we'd both been GI's in the big one. Not that we didn't notice we still had different roles. He had all those rules, regulations and politicos up the ladder. I was answerable only to my clients and my conscience, and that gave me a lot more room to maneuver.

"Captain Butler here."

"Steve, it's Casey."

"How could I be so lucky? It's hit the fan all day long, and here you are…wanting a favor I bet."

"Boy, it's nice to know that being a captain hasn't changed your personality. And yeah, I do need a favor. I'm headed up east to chat with a minor pug and thought I ought to get an intro into the neighborhood precinct in case we get loud."

"What are you doing up in that part of the city?" I gave him the short version and told him Chiquita was working the background of the Home.

"We've had a couple of looks at that place, but never made anything stick. Tell you what, Casey, I'll make the call on the condition that you keep me informed. A couple of the beat cops up there trained with us when they came out of Academy. That doesn't mean you get a pass no matter what. Don't make me sorry I made the call."

"You know me, Steve, I'll be in touch."

He said something about knowing me and my ancestry, and we both hung up laughing.

Like I said, Steve was a good cop. Plus he married a cop's daughter, and they produced another cop's daughter about six months ago. I got one of the cigars and helped him kill a bottle of Jack Daniels whiskey in celebration.

I automatically checked the coin drop and was rewarded with a nickel. It took about fifteen minutes to reach Chen's Cleaners. It was in the middle of the block with nondescript stores on both sides and across the street. I strolled down the other side of the street to get a feel for the block. I paused at a window where I could watch the cleaners in the reflection, and by the time I made the loop, I had seen three hoods that I tabbed as numbers runners go in and come back out and one goon that went in and didn't come back out. He was in a suit, but didn't have a tailor and it was easy to spot the bulge of his shoulder holster.

Chen's door was propped open to catch the spring air, but as soon as I stepped in, I was enveloped in laundry heat and the smell of cleaning fluid. A Chinese girl materialized behind the counter. Her long black hair was pulled back tight and her skin had a sheen from the heat. Her eyebrows were two perfect arches over inquiring Asian eyes. The counter didn't hide the sensuous cling of her dress.

"Hep you sir?"

"I'm here to see Joey." The eyebrows went a little higher.

"You name?"

"Casey Stone. Tell him I'm from Downtown with a message for him alone."

I watched as she turned and walked quickly down an aisle beside a row of hanging cleaning to a door with a peephole. It was a pleasure to watch her move. She rapped twice, and then spoke quietly through the crack. It closed as she came back and motioned me toward the aisle. As I stepped by her, she whispered—"Cahful," and held three fingers up against the top of her dress.

I gave a tiny nod and strode to the door, knowing I was being watched. It swung open before I could knock. The big guy that needed a tailor held it open while I walked in. His broad pasty face was blank as he gave me the once over and said in a flat voice, "He's carrying, boss." He shut the door behind me and stepped back to the left.

"He's right, I am," I said, taking a seat uninvited in the high backed brown chair facing the desk.

Joey was a smallish guy with a ferret face and slicked-back hair seated behind the polished mahogany desk. He had a tailor, but it didn't do him much good. Even with fancy duds, he still looked like a street punk.

The third guy was in the right hand corner behind me. Tall, slender, unmoving in a white suit, he had the air of a cat poised to leap. Pasty Face may have been a foot soldier, long on muscle and short on smarts, but Slim made up for it, I guessed.

The goons were both behind me on opposite sides of the room. I knew it, and I didn't care. I looked at Joey, tapped

13

out a coffin nail and lit up. The ferret had his elbows on his chair arms with his fingers tented below his chin. "Casey Stone. The one I've read about in the papers a few times? Charged with manslaughter?"

"The same, but I beat it," I acknowledged, flicking my ash in his marble ashtray. I enjoyed watching the wheels turn in his eyes. He looked just like the kind of creep that would put the arm on a girl like Rose. The room was nice: good carpet, walls insulated enough to keep sound in or out, a couple of paintings of the old country and several black and white family photos on the walls.

"Nice place you've got here. Kind of ironic, running your dirty business out of a cleaners." Pasty stirred; Slim never moved.

Joey's eyes narrowed and his voice squeezed through gritted teeth. "Girl said you had a message for me."

"If she told you right, she said it was for you alone, and three's a crowd." I made it a point to look Pasty over and then Slim. Pasty was big and thick and mean, and those battering rams he called fists were covered with scars. Slim might have been a statue, but his eyes met mine with a glitter.

"They stay here, Stone, but you'd better go."

"Not until I've done my duty, Joey."

"Mr. Catalano to you, Buster," Pasty said stepping toward my chair.

I didn't wait for him to get to me. I spun out of the chair and put my cigarette out on his cheek. He jerked back with a startled yelp interrupted by a loud "whoof" as I buried my fist in his belly. As he fell to his knees, I snapped his head back with my left knee. He thudded to the floor on his back without another sound.

I read Slim right. He hadn't moved but was tensed waiting for Joey's signal. We all froze for a moment, then Joey, mouth working before any sound came out, hate streaming from his eyes, said, "Felix, take care of Sam. Close the door behind you and be back in five minutes flat. Our guest will be leaving by then."

14

Felix the cat moved soundlessly to his buddy who was just beginning to move. He helped him stumble to his feet and walked him out. The big lunk wasn't going to be kissing any babies for a while. His nose was all over his face. I watched them out the door as Slim gave me a parting glare.

Joey had his hands below the surface of the desk when I spun around. I fanned my .45 out before he could move.

"Hands on the desk, Joey." He may have had the name of a tough guy, but he turned green and broke a sweat looking at my cannon four feet away. He carefully laid his hands on the desk. I had to hand it to him, he put on a good show, green or not.

"You've got about four minutes now, PI. You'd better make it quick."

"It won't take me long, tough guy. I know about Rose. I know about her kid. I know about the trust. You need to forget about all three when I walk out that door. If I have to come back, the only message I'm bringing is this." I let him look at my automatic for another heartbeat, then backed carefully to the door, took a quick glance through the peephole and slipped out pulling it closed behind me.

I quick-stepped past the cleaning, but there was no sign of Slim and his baggage. The girl stood wide-eyed at the counter as I slipped Betsy back into my holster.

"You come back for cleaning spesel?" she said, a bit too loud, pushing a coupon with some handwriting on it across the counter. I shouldn't have been surprised that Joey had the front wired.

"Thanks, babe. Maybe so," palming the coupon into my right pocket while leaving her a business card and a wink. I think I was rewarded with a smile, but like they say, those Orientals are inscrutable. After a quick glance up and down the street, I headed back toward Manny's, careful to stop a couple of times to check for tails.

Chapter 4

Mid-afternoon at Manny's was quiet. There were just a couple of guys arguing ward politics over a cup of joe, and Manny checking register tapes in the same back booth we'd shared two hours ago. He looked up. "You again?" I told him about my visit with Joey.

"Yeah, Sam Napolitano is old muscle the mob put with Joey to keep an eye on him. I don't know anything about that Felix guy except he don't drink, don't use drugs, and don't like girls. They say he's out of Miami. Been up here about a month."

He pointed me to the phone booth in the back, and I used my free nickel to call the office. This time Chiquita chirped the office hello on the first ring.

"It's me, Chick. Whatcha got for me?"

She chattered like a string of Fourth of July firecrackers. "Where you been boss? I really caught a break. I called my girlfriend at City Hall Business License. She looked up everything they had on The Home. She checked taxes, fire, food, utility and electrical inspections. She called her friend at State. It turns out that The Home was started by a lawyer back in the 20's as a charity because he lost his daughter to a botched abortion and wanted to make sure girls had a safe place to go for help. He died about ten years ago...no widow, no kids. Estate went to some nephew nobody's ever seen. All the bills, licenses, everything goes to a CPA not two blocks from our office, by the name of Simon Rosenthal. Not bad for one day's work, huh boss?"

"Not bad at all!! What's Rosenthal's address?" I wrote down his address and phone number.

"So, what have you got for me, boss?"

"You mean besides good looks, winning personality, and lots of love?"

"Can it, boss. I've been working my tail off for this kid and all you've got is cute?" She was actually a bit peeved.

"O.K., O.K., I've been on the job too." I told her about Manny, my chat with Steve, and my visit with Joey and his goons. "And, Chick," *she hated that nickname*, "if I get a call from a Suzie Oh, make sure I hear about it pronto."

"Oh, 'Suzie Oh,'" she singsonged. "What does she have to do with anything?" I didn't have to see her to know that her right hand was on her waist, long red fingernails drumming on her three-inch wide patent leather belt.

"She's the girl at the cleaners. She tried to help and may help again. I think she knows a lot, and I slipped her a business card."

"What does she look like?"

"Not that it should matter to you, nosy senorita, but she's a real China doll."

I told her to close the office and go home when she'd finished opening the mail and be there promptly at 9:00 the next morning.

I hung up, and turned around to see Manny laughing silently at me. "You're a real crowd pleaser, ain't you, Detective?"

I told him to stick it in his ear and reminded myself to shut the phone booth door next time.

I caught the subway downtown and ducked into Pat's for a beer before I went to the office to check the calls and the mail. I figured the mail was mostly bills anyway and it was nice to be ahead on the bar tab.

It was after 6:00 when I stuck the key in the lock and pushed open the old oak door with the etched glass panel and stepped inside. Familiar odors of old leather furniture, old cigarettes, and old building surrounded me. As I walked toward Chiquita's desk, I deliberately inhaled deeply, searching the odors for her floral scent. I usually could guess how long she'd been gone by how faint the aroma. She didn't know I played that game and was always peeved if I guessed when she had left.

In mid-breath, I caught something different and grabbed Betsy from my shoulder holster and thumbed off the safety. Nothing looked out of place on her desk, but the scent was stronger as I turned toward my office—exotic, delicate, jasmine. I flattened against my doorjamb and whirled inside in a crouch, gun sweeping the room.

Suzie jumped. She had been sitting on my old sofa, hands folded in her lap, ankles crossed. She was in a black sheath with ornate embroidery. The high collar hugged her neck and a slit rose high on both sides of her skirt. She smelled of jasmine.

"You scah me."

"How did you get in, Suzie?

"You gullfend let me in and say you be late. She also say you have disease and not to touch."

I laughed until I collapsed across my desk, tears streaming down my face, gasping for breath, still holding Betsy, but fortunately with the safety back on. Finally, I could talk.

"Suzie, she's not my girlfriend…she's my secretary and she's jealous. You know jealous?"

She nodded yes.

"And the only disease I have is falling in love with every beautiful woman I meet."

"She wohied about you and me?"

"Yes, she is."

"Meybe she wight."

I sank into my chair and looked at her. "Maybe she is." It might not qualify as a disease, but I could get lovesick over her real quick. I tossed my hat on the desk and asked why she was here.

"I know you spesel guy when you come in cleaners today. Most people scared. You no scared and you beat up Sam. Joey velly mad when you leave. Joey bad man. He tell my uncle, Fu Chen, he burn down cleaners if he no let Joey have office there. My uncle say he no want gangsters, but Sam hit uncle and run off workers. After two weeks, my uncle say yes. That two year ago. He no pay rent and hurt business. Maybe you make Joey leave?"

I was no Sir Galahad, but making Joey leave would be a pleasure and would fit with my job. "Suzie, I'm working on a case that just happens to involve Joey. Maybe I can get rid of him."

I quizzed her about everything that went on. I was right about the numbers. There were four regular runners and a weekly pick up by a hard-faced man that came every Monday. A small hotel two blocks away was home for his stable of ten girls. He had about five drug pushers on the streets. Most of the businesses nearby were paying him protection. It was the ugly side of my city.

I thought I loved blonds: tall, leggy, blue-eyed babes that knew how to show why God created Eve for Adam. As I looked across the desk, I realized I was wrong. In fact, I loved tiny, raven-haired women with black eyes, shy ways, who smelled of jasmine, and turned a simple black embroidered silk sheath into a tantalizing collection of curvy mysteries.

I took her to supper at my favorite Italian restaurant. I figured she got enough Chinese on her own. We ate, we shared a bottle of Chianti. I waved down a cab and took her to my flat. The next thing I knew we were standing at arms-length from each other with nothing on but the radio, softly lit by the glow from the outside world. She stood like a statue with her eyes down—modest, yet unashamed. No sculptor could have chiseled such luminescent beauty.

As I took her face in my hands, she tilted her head up and looked at me. I kissed her forehead, I kissed her nose, I kissed both cheeks, and by the time I got to her lips, I crushed her to me and smothered a little moan from her.

I stroked her hair which reached half-way down her back, leaned down to kiss her neck and was enveloped in the wonder of her scent, and her smooth velvety skin. I lifted that precious body and laid her softly on the bed. She sensed every move I made and met me in perfect harmony.

Our tempo rose and fell and peaked in a crescendo of bodies and souls.

After a space of suspended bliss, she stealthily crept back into my consciousness and led me to a jasmine scented heaven filled with delicate brushes of fragrant hair, touches of exquisite sensation, pangs of sweet delight and joy shot through with bolts of white hot ecstasy beyond all my experience.

I woke long after the moon and stars had settled back into their orbits and turned to look at her in the dimness. She was a vision of swells and curves through light and shadow and her sleeping face floated in a sea of black hair in a larger sea of white linen. I was transfixed by the gentle rise and fall of her breathing which brought her breasts out of the shadows only to sink quietly back into darkness. The dip of her waist swept sharply up to her hip, only to flow down the gentle curve of thigh and calf. It was irresistible. I could not help myself. I ran my fingertips along her silhouette and she breathed a tiny sigh, which ended in a fleeting smile before the sandman took her back.

Chapter 5

I beat Chiquita to the office by an hour, dealt with the mail, paid some bills, made a few calls, and was writing her a note when she walked in.

"Hi, Chick. I just put on a pot of coffee, left you some notes, and I'm off to see that CPA. Hang around here till I get back, then we'll set up an appointment with Rose's lawyer. Great day, isn't it?!" I was out the door and half way down the hall before it hit me that Chiquita had watched me exit without saying a word, mouth hanging open. I was still flying high on the most fantastic night of my life and a wake-up as sweet as sugar candy. If this were love, I'd have another helping. With a chuckle, I wondered if Chick could detect a whiff of jasmine in the air.

I didn't wait for the elevator—I took the two flights of stairs at a run, burst onto the street with a grin and headed west to see Simon Rosenthal.

If I'd been myself, it never would have happened. The front of the car eased silently by me as I heard a pistol safety click off. I dove over the low iron railing marking the building supervisor's sunken entrance, but I wasn't quick enough to avoid the .38 slug, which laid a hot poker along my left side. It spun me over, and I landed on my back, but I drew my Colt and rolled on over into a crouch. All I saw was a glimpse of a white suit coat, exhaust and a Connecticut license plate on the rear of a black Ford sedan. It had to be Slim from Miami. As I stood up, I was enraged at the burning pain under my left arm and the fact that my new suit was headed straight back to Morrie, the tailor.

This was Joey's doing. Maybe Rose and Suzie's prayers would be answered sooner than anybody thought.

When the beat cop came running up, I gave him the Reader's Digest version and told him to make sure Captain Butler knew about it. I turned down a ride to the Belleview ER and headed back up to the office with my handkerchief clamped against my side.

Chiquita had patched me up before and did it again, chattering the whole time about being careful, seeing a doctor, taking a day off, and a lot of other things I should do or should not do. When she paused for breath, I noticed the tears in her eyes and kissed her on the cheek.

"Oh Boss, sometimes I worry so much about you." She finished the bandage, and I tested it with a little twist and caught my breath at the pain. I was lucky the slug didn't crack a rib, but I was going to be pretty sore for a few days. Chiquita helped me get my backup shirt and suit on, scolding me the whole time until I kissed her on the lips as she was buttoning up my shirt. She was so startled she shut up.

"Now, wipe the lipstick off me and run that suit coat to Morrie's to patch those holes. Ask him when it will be ready and remember to pick it up. When you get back, call Steve and give him the full report and tell him I'll check in after I visit the CPA. See if he's heard anything. I need to check out this CPA before Joey finds him and before I get too stiff to move."

I took a couple of aspirin and chased them with a swig of bourbon from a bottle I kept in my lower left desk drawer. Chiquita frowned and said, "Boss, it's too early to be drinking, sore ribs or no."

"Chick, it'll be OK. Now get that coat over to Morrie's."

She took off in a huff. I ran a comb through my hair, left a note on her desk that said, "Thanks," and locked up.

I rode the elevator down this time. The glow from last night had been replaced by blast furnace anger. Simon the CPA had better be talkative. The two-block walk helped clear my head. His office was on the sixth floor right across from the elevator in a seedy yellow brick sixteen story building. His door was just like mine—but instead of lettering, it had a small metal holder for his business card tacked to the wood above the lock. I went in without knocking.

It looked like an accountant's office: two small rooms filled with filing cabinets, a large desk covered with neat piles of invoices underneath paperweights marked "Paid" and "Unpaid." Tape covered with red and black figures spiraled out of an adding machine. A neat row of sharpened yellow pencils was on one side of the desk pad, and on the other side was a neat row of yellow pencils that needed to be sharpened. Behind the desk sat a small man behind rimless glasses in a dingy white shirt with an ancient stain from the Parker fountain pen in his pocket. He had a green eye shade and sleeve garters. I almost pinched myself to check if I had stepped into a long-ago decade. At least the lights were electric instead of gas.

"Mr. Rosenthal?"

He looked up with calculating eyes. "Yes...," he said in a measured voice.

"I'm Casey Stone, PI," I said flashing my ID. I had it halfway back into my pocket when he clucked, "Tut, tut, sir. Let me see it, please." His manner was last century formal, but clearly he was no fool. Handing it back after a careful examination and noting my name, address and phone number plus the date and time on the corner of his desk pad, he fixed his gaze on me and spoke.

"I rarely am favored with a visit from the law enforcement community, Mr. Stone, but such contacts always follow a pattern. You ask for information...I ask for a search warrant; you don't have one...I bid you adieu. Is this visit to be any different?"

The flicker of his smile disappeared when I shoved a pile of "Unpaids" onto the floor and sat on the corner of his desk. I pulled out Betsy, released the full magazine, slowly looked it over, snapped it back into the handle and reupholstered her.

"Yes, Mr. Rosenthal, this visit is going to be different. I do need information, I don't have a search warrant, but you will not bid me adieu until I get the information." I let it sink in while I studied the office. Most of the cabinets had drawers that were neatly labeled with business names in alphabetical order. One set of file cabinets in the back were labeled only by years, starting with 1924.

"This is your lucky day, Mr. Rosenthal. A girl's life is in danger. You have the opportunity to be a good citizen, maybe even a hero. She was born at The Home sixteen years ago." I saw his eyes flick toward the numbered cabinets. "I need to find her before the bad guys do." I gave him the name and date. "Now it's your turn. Simon says look where?"

He started to object, but I lifted him out of his chair by his collar, and he instantly walked to those cabinets. They were all locked, and when he pulled the key ring from his pocket, his hands were shaking so badly he looked like he was flagging a cab. I took the key and unlocked the cabinet he indicated. He pulled out a drawer and thumbed through to a thick manila folder. I pulled it out and opened it on the top of the cabinet. It was filled with receipts, statements, and a green accounting ledger page of credits and debits. I ran my finger down the column of receipts until I found an entry, "Kelly, alias baby girl, $5,000.00, JKM, LI."

"What's 'JKM, LI' mean, Simon?"

"I couldn't tell you if I wished, Mr. Stone. The client always coded such entries, and payments were always in cash. Only they would know." It made sense, and I believed him. I put the folder back in the drawer after slipping the ledger sheet under my coat. I walked him back to his desk and dropped him in his chair.

"You did well, Mr. Rosenthal. It's almost time to bid me adieu, as you say. But I'm not the only one that might visit you about this. There's a lot at stake, and like I said, they're the bad guys. You need to do two things. First, improve your story so they don't get the same information I did; and second, let me know all about it if somebody comes by."

He was still nodding agreement when the elevator doors shut behind me. My side was burning and my ribs were aching, and I decided I was overdue for a break. Besides, I needed to talk to Steve. I called at the first phone booth.

"Butler here."

"Steve, Casey. Where can we talk?"

"Queenie's in fifteen minutes," and he hung up.

Queenie was the secretary to the old precinct Captain and quit when the Captain retired rather than break in a new boss. She had the best eatery in Lower Manhattan. It was just around the corner from the precinct and was probably the safest place to eat in three states, as every customer was on the force and Queenie knew them all by name. She may have retired from the payroll, but she never quit being a cop.

I got there long enough before Steve to order two beers and two daily specials. He slid into the booth just as Queenie set down the glasses.

"Steve, honey, you look a bit frazzled. First one's on me." No wonder she had the best repeat business in the city.

"Thanks, Queenie. It's the company I keep," he said throwing a glare in my direction.

"Hey, pal. This is my treat. Give me a break."

"You're right, Casey," he sighed. "It's been a rough day and a lot of the flack has had your name written all over it."

"Me? I'm the one that's lucky to have sore ribs instead of a free ride to the morgue. What's up?"

He drained half his glass on the first draught. I whistled to Queenie before she got behind the bar, held up two fingers, and she nodded OK.

"Casey, give me the whole story and don't leave anything out."

"Sure, buddy." I started from the beginning and didn't leave anything out except my mystical evening with Suzie. "What do you make of this, 'JKM, LI'? I figure the LI is Long Island, but there must be a hundred JKMs."

Steve downed the last of his beer just as Queenie set down refills, and the waiter handed over our corn beef hash.

He didn't speak till he had downed two big fork loads of hash.

"Casey, you've stirred up something, and I don't know exactly what. Just before I got the report on you getting shot at, I got a call from Headquarters complaining about you throwing your weight around uptown. It doesn't smell right, but I can't figure out how it got back to me so fast."

"Steve, who's this JKM?"

"Well, I think you're right about Long Island. Joseph K. Menaphy...ring any bells?"

"Not to me. Help me out."

"Old money. Big influence. Connections all the way to DC. Doesn't run for officepicks the people who do. Always behind the scenes except at charity functions. Pillar of the community. And get this, he's a big sponsor of The Home."

"Where's his place?"

"Gated estate on the Sound. Private security force that has mob written all over it."

We finished our meal, both lost in thought, left a tip, and waved goodbye to Queenie.

"Steve, I've gotta meet this guy."

Chapter 6

I headed back to the office just to see if anything had happened. It hadn't. I called Carl at the 58th Street Garage where I stored my car and told him to make sure it was gassed up and ready to roll in the morning. Carl was pleased. "'Bout time, Mr. S. Ya know a car needs to run to be able to run. You ain't been drivin' enough to keep her happy."

It was a Ford coupe, one of the first new models after the war. It was nice to look at, but didn't have enough moxie to measure up. A couple of years ago, I was grousing about losing a mark because she couldn't run fast enough when Carl said, "Mr. S., I can make her run right if you want, and it won't cost that much."

Carl was from the East Tennessee hills and had been the mechanic in the family moonshine business till Uncle Sam sent him to Europe to fight the Krauts. He was discharged in New York City and never left.

"Wouldn't take much to make her a real ridge runner, Mr. S. Got a stout V-8 from a wrecked police special that'd fit right in. Course, with that many horses, we'd have to beef up the runnin' gear too."

There weren't any ridges in Manhattan, but it still sounded good, and I told him to do it. By the time he finished, she'd do 130 and handle curves and corners like she was born to it. If I lost a chase after that, it was my fault, not the car's. Ever since then, Carl regarded her as his baby, and I got holy hell if I brought her back with a dent.

I dialed Rose and told her we needed to talk. She said she could be at my office a half hour after she got off work. I had about three hours and called the law firm and asked for Mr. Greenberg. When I asked if I could meet with him about Rose, he was non-committal. "I'm not acquainted with you, Mr. Stone. Nor do I have the right to confirm or deny whether I have a client named Rosemary Kelly.

"My mistake, Mr. Greenberg. You have her work number and she's there, because I just spoke to her. You check, and if she OKs me, can I see you in about thirty minutes?"

He said, "Yes", and I caught the Lexington Avenue Subway to Midtown and walked over to Greenberg's address on Fifth Avenue.

It was a fancy building suitable for a fancy street. The firm had two full floors. The receptionist had auburn hair and was dressed in a two-piece gray suit with a muted plaid scarf tucked in at the neck. She flashed me a smile as she finished a phone call, leaned forward on her elbows and asked, "How may I help you, Sir?"

I started to tell her, but instead flashed my best smile and said, "Mr. Stone, here to see Mr. Greenberg. He's expecting me." She announced me into her switchboard, listened for a response, and then turned to me. "It'll be a moment. Is there anything I can get for you?"

"I noticed a great aroma when I came in. If it wasn't you, was it fresh coffee?" She took the bait and ran with it.

"Good nose, Mr. Stone. It was me, and, I just made some fresh coffee. How do you like it?"

"You, or the coffee?"

"First me and then the coffee."

"I like you just fine, and I like the coffee hot and black."

She wrinkled her nose at me and made a little pout and sashayed down the hallway to the first door, high heels clicking the whole way. Before she ducked in, she looked back over her shoulder to make sure I was watching, and returned in a moment with a large steaming mug on a small

28

tray. She bent over a little closer to me than she had to, to set it down on the tiny end table beside my chair.

"If you don't mind me saying so, Miss…"

"Maureen. It matches the hair," she interrupted.

"If you don't mind me saying so, Maureen, you do more for a gray flannel suit than Hart Schaffner & Marx ever did."

"I don't mind, Big Boy. Thanks for noticing."

Her switchboard buzzed and after a brief exchange, she turned and said, "Follow me, please."

"Anywhere, Babe. It'll be a pleasure."

She gave me another one of those looks, wiggled that suit at me, and led me down the hall to a polished solid oak door with a brass nameplate engraved with, "David Greenberg, Esquire." He was standing as I entered and extended his hand. As we shook, he said, "I hope you will understand my earlier caution, Mr. Stone. My concern was not only attorney/client confidentiality, but in this case, we have the additional concern for the welfare of the primary trust beneficiary."

"That puts us on the same side, Mr. Greenberg. Can I speak in confidence as well?"

"Certainly, Mr. Stone. Miss Kelly gave us carte blanche in our dealings with you. Her very words were, 'Dealing with him, is the same as dealing with me.' What can I do for you?"

"I'm turning up some interesting connections. You know the kid was born at The Home and adopted out—or at least we assume so because Rose signed the papers. I've learned of a $5,000.00 payment by a JKM, probably from Long Island. But Rose says she was underage. Would that void the papers?"

"Perhaps it would, but we still have 16 years' delay in raising the question, and the courts are loathe to overturn longstanding orders. Plus, it's an adoption and those records are sealed."

"That's where you come in, counselor. Isn't there a way to get a judge to unseal them and have a peek?"

He launched into a learned discourse debating with himself about why it was unlikely, yet possible, until I was drowning in legalese.

"Mr. Greenberg, you're talking to a PI. Don't tell me why you can't. I saw your name on the door...you're David. David, the boy who slew Goliath with nothing but a sling. We're just talking about a judge. They may think they're only one step below the golden throne, but you're David, the giant killer. And you're fighting for an innocent girl's life."

He stared at me, silent as a stone, which is tough for a lawyer. The silence was broken only by the ticking of the clock hanging on his wall. I wondered if he was going to throw me out. Instead, I think he remembered why he suffered through three years of law school, the bar exam and the background investigation that checked out every sneeze since grammar school. He drew a breath, straightened his shoulders, adjusted his tie, looked me straight in the eye, and said, "Damn right, Mr. Stone, damn right! We're going to take care of that girl. Give me the details."

Maureen was bending over her switchboard with her back to me as I left. I gave her a little pat on the rear as I passed the desk, and she gave me that face and another wiggle as I let myself out.

I had just enough time to get back to my office and the appointment with Rose.

Chapter 7

It was about 5:30 when Rose walked in to the office, looking as good as she did the first time I saw her. She accepted the cigarette and light with a nod, took the first puff, and then zeroed in. "Mr. Stone, what has my two thousand bucks got me?" Still brassy, still just right to me.

"Well, Miss Kelly, we've done a good deal in two days. Chiquita's checked the city records on The Home, I've met Manny, I had an appointment with your lawyer, I've met that piece of crap, Joey, and I've been shot at by one of his goons."

"I knew I had the right man when you gave me that Camel in our first meeting." A bit of pleading entered her voice. "But are we going to beat the deadline? And is Angel safe?"

I took a deep breath before answering. "Rose, I got to be honest. If they'll shoot at me in broad daylight in Greenwich Village, they'll shoot her without batting an eye. It's still a race."

She took it like a man. After a couple of thoughtful puffs, she stubbed her cigarette out and said, "So where are you taking me to dinner?"

Nigel's Steak House sounded good, and it was. Well done for me, and rare for her. It fit.

"Will you come up for a nightcap?" she said as we got out of the cab. I paused, thinking of last night. "Of course you will," she said waving off the cab and grabbing me by the elbow.

Robert W. Godwin

"Careful," I yelped. "Ribs...sacrificed for the girl."

She held my elbow more gently as we went up the steps. She unlocked the entrance door and walked me to the elevator. At her floor, still holding my elbow, she unlocked her door and led me straight to the sofa. As I laid my hat on the sofa arm, shifted to ease the ribs and took a breath, she stepped to the bar and was back in a moment. "Bourbon, on the rocks...here." She set the glass down in front of me. While I took a sip, then another, she disappeared into the next room and reappeared in a gauzy pink gown held closed only by a ribbon at the neck. As she passed in front of the lamp, I knew it was the only thing she had on.

She knelt in front of me and took a deep sip from a wine glass and rolled it around in her mouth before swallowing. Her eyes never left me, and she languidly licked her lips before she spoke. "I'm more comfortable, how about you?"

Before I could answer, she grabbed my tie and pulled me forward. She met my lips hard, tongue probing my mouth, her other hand releasing my belt.

The rush of passion swept over me. I pressed her lips hard against mine. The taste of Chardonnay mixed with the salty tang of blood from a crushed lip. When we had to breathe, gasping I pushed her back on the rug and her gown fluttered to either side of her except where it was held together by the ribbon at the neck. She made no effort to pull it closed, but deliberately leaned back on her elbows, boldly gazing up at me.

I ripped off my clothes ignoring the throbbing ribs and dropped to the floor, my knees capturing both thighs and a hand pinning each of her wrists to the floor. She never flinched, but raised a challenging eyebrow over a little smile. I bent down to her belly, inhaled her fragrance, and then kissed her lightly on each side in the little valley above her hips. She let out a long, low groan as I worked my way up to her ribs, then along the underside of her right breast, pushing the gown aside with my face. Her eyes glittered, and she caught her breath sharply as I lightly brushed her nipple on the way to the bow.

I took the end of a ribbon in my teeth and slowly began to pull, rising to her open lips. As the bow parted, I let the ribbon drop from my teeth and dodged her hungry lunge for a kiss. Instead, I ducked under her chin to her creamy throat and nibbled back to her left breast. I never loosed my grip on her wrists, which were quivering as I paused over that wondrous mound. Her breath became raspy and each pant was a half-uttered "please."

At last, I could wait no longer and released her wrists and crushed her body to me. As we fused together, she bit my shoulder. We rolled back and forth on the floor, yelps of pleasure and pain filling the air, until at last, we lay still amid tatters of pink gauzy gown, with no sound but gasping breath, slowly subsiding into measured quiet and sleep.

I woke with an ache in my left side and a twinge in my conscience. I slipped out from under Rose's arm, found my clothes and eased out the door without waking her. It was predawn in the city, when garbage was on the way out and freshness was on the way in. I made my way home and fell asleep across my bed fully dressed.

Sore ribs and the mid-morning sun woke me as I rolled over. I took a hot shower, shaved, dressed and headed to the office. Suzie had called while I was with Rose, and I was stricken with guilt. I dialed her number, and she answered on the second ring.

"Suzie, it's me."

"I miss you yesterday."

"That's two of us, Doll."

"Joey acting funny at me."

I leaned forward and clutched the phone, "How, funny?"

"He look at me long time when he come in and whisper to Felix. Then Felix look hard at me too."

"Suzie, can Uncle Chen cover the counter without you?"

"Yes, I think so."

"OK. Tell him you are going to the ladies room, but go out the back door and use the key I gave you to get into my flat. Call Uncle once you are there and tell him you are sick and won't be back for a few days and hang up. Don't tell him where you are. Will you do that?"

"Yes, Mr. Casey. I will do what you say."

"Good. Be careful. I'll see you tonight."

I couldn't stand the thought of Joey, or Sam, or Felix with their hands on her. I sat there mentally kicking myself for underestimating Joey. If he was going to stake out my office and have Felix take a potshot at me, he probably knew about Suzie coming to see me.

Chiquita arrived all smiles, till she saw me. "What's wrong, Boss?" I bit the bullet and told her that Joey must have figured out that Suzie was giving me the lowdown on his operation, and I was going to hide her at my place for a few days until I could get things sorted out.

Green flashes from those pretty eyes replaced the smiles. "How convenient. How noble. You burn me up Mr. Stone!"

"Listen, if they'll shoot at me, you know what they'll do to her, and they've got her right at their doorstep at the cleaners. I had to do something."

This time I didn't have to imagine the hand on the hip and the drumming fingers. She glared at me until I finally lit a cigarette. Still glaring, she said, "I talked to my brother, Jesus, last night. He works for a catering business that does a lot of fancy parties on Long Island. He's been to the Menaphy mansion for stag parties. There are big walls around the estate and guards at the gate. He says there are always several girls there, but they aren't treated like daughters. Mr. Menaphy hands them out to guests who are spending the night. Some of them are as young as Miss Kelly's kid."

She had my attention.

"And that's not all. My mother's sister works for a cleaning company that services The Home. She sees and hears a lot of things. She says a Mr. Menaphy comes by often, and they treat him like he owns the place. He goes over the list of girls that are there and sometimes talks to them and takes them away after they have their babies. Sometimes he takes the babies, always the girl babies. She heard the headmistress talking to the secretary about Mr. Menaphy having a dormitory and nursery at his place, but they stopped talking as soon as they saw her. When I asked Jesus about any other buildings at the mansion, he said the catering staff was forbidden to leave the big house, but he knew there were other buildings on the property that he thought were servants' quarters, because he saw children down there. He doesn't remember seeing any boys, just girls."

I listened, but couldn't believe what I was hearing. The guy was a farmer—raising and harvesting human flesh for consumers right here under our noses, in the land of the free and the home of the brave. So this is what we licked the Krauts and the Japs for; so garbage like this could run loose. I don't know what showed on my face, but Chiquita looked frightened.

"Chick, I've got to meet this guy and see for myself what that place looks like. But I need a cover to get past the gate. Let's see if Greenberg is worth anything. Get him on the phone." Things were rolling around so fast in my mind, Chiquita had to yell twice, "Got him, Boss."

"Mr. Greenberg, do you think you could get me a meeting with Mr. Menaphy? I need to look around his place and security is tighter than Fort Knox. I couldn't pull it off pretending I had money, but you could tell him I'm a local security man for an out-of-towner coming to establish a New York office. Somebody who wants to get in good with local heavyweights. Somebody wanting a visible charity to build some goodwill."

"How soon do you want in, Mr. Stone?"

"Today, if possible. Things are moving pretty fast."

"I'll see what I can do, Mr. Stone. I'll call you back as soon as I can."

I gave Carl a ring to have the car up front so I could get it at a moment's notice. I broke out my maps and figured out how to get to Great Neck, Long Island, not an area I was used to visiting. I calculated it would take an hour and a half, and that was if the bridges weren't backed up. Then I worked on my story. It had to be good, because the guy would have it checked before I got back out of his gate:

somebody with new money, a common name, maybe from Canada.

I was too antsy to think clearly and decided to clean Betsy. I spread an oilcloth on my desk, got the Hoppe's kit and had her apart, cleaned, oiled, and back together when the phone rang. I heard Chick say, "Yes, sir, he's right here," and picked up the extension before she could call to me.

"Mr. Stone?" Came Mr. Greenberg's voice with a triumphant note. "You are expected at Menaphy's at 3:00 PM sharp. You will have one-half hour, no more. His appointments secretary was rather brusque, but the firm name got you in. They know nothing except your name and what you outlined to me earlier."

"David," I said, "you look good in a tunic with a sling. Maybe together we can load that sling with a pebble or two and bring Goliath down." He laughed and said, "Good hunting, Mr. Stone."

As soon as I cradled the receiver, the phone rang again. After a cheery hello, Chick's tone turned cold as she called to me. "For you. I'm going to the powder room."

I picked up. "Stone here." Ah ha! It was Suzie. "Did you make it to my place OK?" She had, and she was sure she hadn't been followed. She also noted that my place needed cleaning up and there were dirty dishes in the sink.

"Yeah, well…Suzie, I have to run out to Long Island. I ought to be back by 6:00 and will come straight there, but don't open the door unless you hear my voice. Understand? And throw both security bolts as soon as you hang up. Don't answer the phone. If I or Chiquita call you, we'll let it ring twice, hang up, and then call right back."

"Yes, Mr. Casey."

"And, Suzie, you can drop that Mr."

"Yes, Mr. Casey, sir."

"Suzie!" I said with irritation only to hear her dissolve in a flood of giggles.

Chapter 8

Chiquita was in a slightly better mood when she came back from the powder room. I told her about Mr. Greenberg's arrangements, that Suzie had made it to my apartment OK, and the telephone code we would use. She said she wouldn't be calling Suzie. I slipped Betsy into my holster and told Chick to phone Carl.

He had just topped off the tank when I got there. It was good to get in and just drive. After I crossed the East River, I worked over to the Long Island Expressway and headed north. I got to the fancy area a bit early and drove on past Menaphy's to get a feel for this part of the Island. Everybody had a fence or a wall and the gates were a mile apart. I came back in time to make my appointment and pulled up to the gate. Menaphy really liked his initials. They were three feet high in the middle of a huge iron bar gate that blocked the drive between large brick pillars. The pillars anchored nine-foot high brick walls on either side.

As I pulled up, a man that could have been Pasty Face's younger brother stepped out of the guardhouse and approached the gate while another one waited in the doorway. They were in uniform and both wore Sam Browne belts with police .38s in shiny black holsters. I had no doubt there was heavier artillery in the guardhouse.

"William N.," I said eyeing his nametag. "I have a 3 p.m. appointment with Mr. Menaphy.

"ID, please," he said checking it against notes on his clipboard. Apparently I was on the approved list, as he handed it back and delivered my instructions. "Stay on the main road. Do not exceed 20 miles an hour. When you reach the mansion, do not stop at the main entrance, but continue to the next door, stop in the first parking place and leave the keys in the ignition. Understand?"

I gave him my best G.I. salute and spit out, "Yes, sir!" He didn't laugh. The gate opened just enough to clear my Ford, and I drove slowly down the drive. I watched in my rearview mirror as William N. wrote down my license plate number.

Manny said Pasty Face was Sam Napolitano. "William N."—to look like Sam, with the same last initial, working for an outfit with mob connections was too much to be coincidence. He had my full ID, but there was no reason to believe that he had any word from big brother on me. Still, I had been careless once and was lucky to get away with only sore ribs.

The main house was turn of the century robber baron style: three story brick mimicking a French Chateau with a slate roof and leaded glass windows. The great expanse of lawn extended hundreds of yards to either side and sloped down to the Sound. On the right was a detached eight-door garage with a second story, which appeared to be living quarters. It probably had been the stable house a few decades ago.

The brown pebble drive made a graceful arc past the huge double doors of the main entrance and at the far end of the house was a door with a small bronze sign that said "Office." As I parked, I could see another substantial building 300 yards to the south, which echoed the style of the main house, but was newer. The drive that led to it had signs on either side that said, "Do Not Enter." A corner of a fenced playground on the backside was visible.

I parked and took my keys with me despite William N's instructions. Nobody was going to drive my car.

I entered the office door and a man behind the desk rose and said, "Very prompt, Mr. Stone. Please come with me." I glanced at the large wall clock as we walked through a heavy wooden door that shut with a quiet whoosh behind us.

Alias Baby Girl

I was five minutes early. I could've had a smoke, but there was no ashtray in sight.

He led me silently up a long hall with several offices on either side, obviously the business wing of Menaphy Enterprises. The door at the end of the hall opened into a large sunroom with floor to ceiling glass windows facing the Sound, and we continued through an open French door to the veranda.

"Please be seated," he said indicating a large round glass table with four ornate iron chairs with cushions. "Mr. Menaphy will be with you shortly."

As he withdrew, I walked to the marble railing and took in the view. A hefty red-faced man in a valet outfit appeared pushing a service cart of drinks. "What can I offer you, sir?" I declined, and he withdrew to the far side of the veranda. I figured I wouldn't see Menaphy until his security guys checked out my ID and license plate. Nobody had offered to take my hat, and it was clear I wouldn't be here long.

It was a magnificent scene. The perfect lawn flowed down to the water's edge where a pure white pier extended into the choppy water. A 90-foot yacht was moored on the left side with sails furled under rich blue covers. On the opposite side was a brick boathouse that matched the style of the other buildings. Although the doors were closed, I pictured a thirty foot teak speedboat powered by a huge inboard V-8 floating quietly inside.

To the left, I could easily see the other house and playground. Twenty people could live there, I guessed. There were a few children running about inside the iron bar fence, watched by a white-clad nanny. Between the two houses were a tennis court and swimming pool separated by a building with dressing rooms for both.

Distant brick walls enclosed the property running all the way to the water's edge where they were replaced by sharp rock jetties topped with barbed wire. Trees were sprinkled about the grounds, but didn't offer much cover if you were trying to move unseen at night. In addition to the flood lights at the pool and tennis court, I could see some on the far house, some on the corners of the main house above the veranda, and several on the pier and boathouse. They could light this place like Yankee Stadium.

My thoughts were interrupted by a soft, almost feminine voice. "Do sit down, Mr. Stone."

"Beautiful view, Mr. Menaphy," I said turning toward him. We shook and his grip was surprisingly firm. He was about seventy, with fine silver hair brushed straight back revealing parchment-colored skin that showed only faint lines. His pale blue eyes, straight nose, and white teeth completed the image of a patrician born to and easy with great wealth. The picture was marred by thin lips that settled into a cruel line. He wore a pale blue silk shirt echoing his eyes, open at the neck with a light gray linen sport coat.

"Were you offered refreshment?"

"Yes, thanks, but I'm here on business, and I know I have limited time."

"Quite so, Mr. Stone. I appreciate your directness. I understand you are the security man for an out-of-town industrialist?"

Steve had done some background checking for me and my story would hold for a while. "His name is Ansil Cooper from Vancouver. He made a bundle during the war supplying the Allies parts for jeeps and tanks. Since the war, he's continued to do well with automotive supply and wants to establish a New York office. He wanted local security for his visit and asked the law firm that handles his US affairs for a recommendation. Fortunately, they remembered some work I had done for them and put us in touch." I paused. "He very much wants to get off on the right foot in New York City. When I asked the law firm for a reference to a prominent, respected local figure, they suggested you and got me the introduction, for which I am very grateful, sir. Mr. Cooper doesn't like publicity, but wants to meet the right people to do business with. He says it never hurts to make a donation to a worthy cause, particularly if it gets noticed by the ones who count. Mr. Greenberg said you would have good advice."

"When will your Mr. Cooper be in New York?"

"In about a month, Mr. Menaphy. As I said, he's a very private person." I deliberately paused, then jumped in. "I'm also supposed to tell you that he expects to combine pleasure with business while here, discreetly of course, and to mention that his taste in women is well portrayed in that book, *Lolita*."

"Mr. Stone! How dare you! I am not a procurer." His face flushed, and he rose from his chair.

"Mr. Menaphy," I said scrambling up, "I apologize. I told Mr. Cooper I didn't want to bring that up, but he said if I wanted the job, I'd have to take orders. He said a man with your connections and experience could steer him in the right direction. People in your circles know a lot of things the public never knows, and that's what he meant. I'm just doing my job."

He stood looking at me long enough for several gulls to circle his yacht and settle on the boathouse.

Finally, he spoke. "Mr. Stone, I spoke harshly a moment ago. I will not condemn you for doing your job. I am always interested in mutually advantageous business arrangements. I do have my favorite charities. I will meet your Mr. Cooper and if everything goes well, it is quite possible that he will return home with exceptional memories of his visit. You may make further contacts with my secretary, Mr. Sanford. Good day, Mr. Stone." He turned on a very expensive heel and disappeared into the house, as Mr. Sanford appeared in response to some secret signal.

Sanford led me back down the hall, handed me a business card with day and night numbers as we passed through his office. He watched from his door until I had passed the turn to the other residence and headed toward the gate.

I glanced at my watch—one-half hour to the minute. The gate rolled open as I approached, and I waved goodbye to William N. He didn't wave back. I turned south and headed back to Manhattan trying to figure out how to get a look inside that dormitory.

Chapter 9

Menaphy had put on a good act. After the indignant reaction, he threw out a clear come-on. That's where I had Steve beat. There was nothing a cop and DA could do with a comment like that, but I could read the handwriting on the wall. Still I wanted to bounce this whole thing off Steve. I was getting lots of leads, but they were just loose ends that I couldn't knot up yet. I really needed to get that adoption file unsealed and see who was who and if Menaphy was the right guy, even though my gut nailed him for a piece of slime.

The city lights were on as I crossed the Queensborough Bridge and headed for the garage. Carl was still there. "How'd she run, Mr. S.?"

"Slick as a greased pig. Is that good hillbilly talk?"

"It ain't good enough to fool nobody, but its purty good for a Yankee."

"Hey, watch your mouth. Yankees live another state or two north of here." He laughed as I turned the car over to him, and he drove it back to storage.

With a good feeling, I headed south to the office. I let myself in, sniffed the air for Chick's fragrance and looked at her notes—nothing important there. I kicked my feet up on my desk and dialed Steve's home number. Janie picked up.

"Hey Beautiful, it's Casey. How 'bout going out with me tonight if we can dump that guy you live with?"

In between giggles, she said, "Sure, but we'll have company anyway, baby Patricia Anne," who I could hear gurgling in her arms.

I'll think about it. Is the babysitter available?"

"Here he is," she said, and handed the phone off still laughing. Steve answered with a huff.

"This better be important, Casey. I'm off duty."

"Cops and dads are never off duty, Pal. I just talked to one of your bosses and heard the other one in the background. I won't take long, but I need your input, Steve. Here's the deal." I brought him up to date on Rose, Lawyer Greenberg and his help in getting me in the gate, the look-alike William N., the Menaphy estate, my talk with Menaphy, and his parting come-on. "What can we do to squeeze that guy?"

"Whoa, slow down Casey. Let's take it step by step. First, your girl was underage when she signed the baby away. Your mouthpiece says we might make some points there, but it's a toughie after sixteen years and the records are sealed anyway. Second, Menaphy may or may not be our guy. We haven't confirmed that through The Home or court records. Third, even if Menaphy has developed a private stable of girls for himself and his guests, we're a long way from proof. Who's going to rat him out by admitting he was bedding an underage girl at any of his parties? Fourth, remember Menaphy's reputation. If somebody even points a finger at him, they'll be swamped by a chorus of reputable citizens singing Menaphy's virtues. Fifth, you've stirred up the mob with Joey Catalano uptown, and I've been getting heat from the top. If Menaphy's guard service is mob connected, and if that was Sam Napolitano's brother you saw at the gate, your ass is in a crack more than Menaphy's."

"Any ideas on how to put the screws to this guy?"

"Pin some underage girl to him."

"Steve, that dormitory is 300 yards away from the main house and security for the entire estate is tighter than a tourniquet."

Robert W. Godwin

"So, what else do you want from me on a late Tuesday evening when Patricia Anne is screaming her head off for a bottle?"

"Nothing else, Pal. Give her a kiss for me and thanks for the help."

I hung up and looked at my worn shoes on the desk. They were $45.00 gumshoe specials. Menaphy would spend more than that on a sneeze into a handkerchief. How was I going to crack him? If Greenberg couldn't get those court records unsealed, it looked like a break and enter at The Home.

I noticed the wall clock. It was 6:45. I dialed my apartment, let it ring twice, hung up and dialed again. The receiver was picked up, but no answer. "Suzie, it's me."

"Oh, Casey, I was getting so wohried."

"No problem, girl. Anything happen while I was gone?"

"Not much. Several times the phone ring and ring, but I no answer."

"What did you do all day?"

"I clean up. You TV not so hot."

"Yeah, I know."

"And somebody come to the door, but I stay quiet."

"Good girl!" My voice was cheery, but this was bad. Nobody got past the Super's door. I'd done him a favor a few years ago when his nephew got in trouble, and he had instructions that nobody was welcome unless I'd given him the OK. "Suzie, I'll pick up some carry-out and be there in a half hour."

When I got to my building, I stopped by the Super's apartment and was relieved to find that he had been up to check the kitchen radiator I had complained about two weeks ago. He heard the TV and thought I was there. I told him Suzie would be hiding out at my place for a few days and had a key. He promised to keep a close eye on visitors for me, and I took him up to meet her. I knocked on the door and told Suzie it was me. When she opened it, I introduced Luther to her, and Suzie got his phone number in case she couldn't get hold of me.

44

As soon as the door closed behind him, Suzie reached her arms up around my neck, pulled me down and kissed me firmly on the lips. "Hi, Casey."

"Hi, Suzie." My heart flooded with relief at her safety and the delight of holding this beautiful jasmine-scented creature close to me. I gazed into those eyes and almost fell in. I kissed her back, and she gave me one of those sweet smiles. I gave her another peck and said softly, "The Moo Goo Gai Pan is getting cold."

She didn't let go. "We can heat it up later, Mr. Stone, sir." She giggled, a sound that I had come to treasure. With her arms still around my neck, I bent over and wrapped an arm around her tiny waist, lifted her off her feet and walked over to the kitchen counter. I set the take-out bag down and with her feet still a foot off the floor, threw my hat on the sofa and carried her giggling to the bedroom.

We reheated supper in the oven and sat on the floor at the coffee table. My bathrobe swallowed her. Shiny black hair fell across her shoulders and down her back. Pink tinged her cheeks. We ate and talked.

I had no trouble with the egg drop soup. The chopsticks were a bigger challenge. I finally laid down my chopsticks with a muttered oath and got a fork from the kitchen drawer. This time at least Suzie tried to hide the giggles behind a hand over her mouth. When we were full, we cuddled up on the sofa with her leaning back against my chest and chatted about everything and nothing, sometimes just listening to each other's breathing.

The phone rang. I jumped up from the sofa and answered, "Stone here."

"Casey...Steve. Simon Rosenthal was killed at his office sometime today. I'm at the scene. You need to get down here right away."

"I'm on the way." While I dressed, I hurriedly told Suzie about my visit with the CPA and what Steve had just said. I grabbed my hat and was reminding her to throw the locks, not answer the door, or the phone, when she gently pushed me out and said, "I know, Casey. Come back quick." She blew me a kiss through the crack as I pushed the door shut.

Chapter 10

I was riding up the elevator in Simon's building in 15 minutes. As the doors opened on the sixth floor, the din struck me. Two uniforms guarded the office door that already had yellow crime scene tape across it. Two reporters were popping flashbulbs and questions at the same time. Captain Butler was in the middle barking orders to everybody in sight, including me as soon as he heard the elevator ding.

"In here, Stone!"

"Stone?" the reporters chorused. "Casey Stone? The P.I. that's been in so much trouble? What's your connection with all this?"

Steve pushed me under the tape into the CPA's office and slammed the door behind us. Simon's office was a mess. His desk was a shambles, file drawers were open and some had contents dumped on the floor. What was left of Simon Rosenthal, CPA, was slumped back in his chair with blood spatters all over the wall behind him. There was a bullet hole in his forehead. The Medical Examiner was bending over him and a plain-clothes cop was knee deep in the files trying to make sense of the mess.

Steve crooked his finger at me and said, "Look at this." He pointed to the corner of Simon's desk pad where he'd noted my visit. Beside his neat lettering was a bold scrawl. "Clock's ticking, Stone."

The ME looked up over the desk at Steve. "Captain, they worked him over pretty good before the fatal shot.

He's got some fractured ribs and fingers too. This has mob written all over it." I looked at Steve. "It has to be Joey and his thugs. They're the only ones beside Rose who care about the one month limit to find the girl."

My list of reasons to get Joey was getting longer by the minute and every time it did, the longer it was going to take for him to die. I was enjoying the thought of him squirming when Steve whispered to me. "Casey, we've got to count on them getting everything out of him that he knew. If it was Joey's people, that means Sam was in the middle of it, which also means they'll make the connection with Menaphy before too long. They'll love that, if we're right about your William N. being Sam's brother."

The uniforms had told him that nobody saw anything and nobody heard anything; the janitor service called the cops. Steve opened the office door and walked the two reporters toward the front of the building, telling them nothing they didn't already know. I slipped down the back stairs unnoticed. At the street level, I ducked out the service entrance and saw two sets of footprints down the alley—one set big and wide; the other long and narrow. It was dark, but the streetlights gave just enough light to follow them. They split to either side of the alley and stopped where they got in a car, likely a Ford sedan with Connecticut plates.

I wasn't good company when I got back to my apartment. I sat in the dark at my kitchen table alternating slugs of bourbon and drags on cigarettes, stewing in frustrated fury. Silently, Suzie came up and began to rub my shoulders and neck. Light and feathery at first, then with increasing strength until all the strings let go, and I laid my head on my crossed arms on the table. Her fingers found every knot and twist up and down my back. She even eased the sore ribs. Finally, she lifted my head and said, "Come on, Casey," and walked me into the bedroom where I fell into a sleep filled with leering devils and young girls running in panic, but never escaping.

I awoke to the smell of frying bacon and eggs and stumbled out of bed. When I stuck my head around the corner, Suzie was standing there with a large glass of tomato juice that I gratefully took.

"Shower and come back. It almost ready."

I did as told, reappearing just as Suzie set my plate down beside my favorite mug full of steaming coffee. I nodded gratefully, dug in, and was into my second cup of coffee before I asked, "How'd you know this was my favorite mug?"

"All others clean," she said matter-of-factly.

"Oh."

"You have many bad dreams. About the girl you look for?"

"Yeah. I've got to find her before Joey does, and he's catching up to me and maybe getting ahead." I downed the last of my coffee and grabbed my hat off the sofa. "I've got to go. Remember..." she held up both hands finishing my sentence..."Door locks, don't open till I hear you, don't answer phone unless two rings...."

"OK, OK, I get it," this time holding up my hands with a laugh. I kissed the tip of her nose and waited outside the door until I heard the bolts slide home. "Bye, China Doll," I whispered through the door.

Robert W. Godwin

Chapter 11

As soon as I got to the office, I checked the mail and Chiquita's notes. I called Greenberg's office. Maureen recognized my voice before I could identify myself and said, "Mr. Greenberg isn't in yet, Mr. Stone. He had an early morning chambers conference at court and should be here about 10 o'clock. He said to be sure and get a number where he could reach you."

"Office, Red. Thanks."

There was a note that Manny had called. When he picked the phone up, I could hear the griddles and cash register going full tilt.

"Manny, it's Casey. I just now saw that you called."

He covered the phone, and I could barely hear him say, "Yesterday a customer asked real casual-like if anybody knew where that girl Rose was these days. It was some broad claiming to be an old classmate of hers. She didn't ask me, she was chatting up the griddle cook. Fortunately, he's been with me twenty years and knows the score. He played dumb and told me about it as soon as he could. The dame was neat and well spoken. She looked like she might work in a high tone business or was an executive secretary. Kind of fancy for my place though, and looked a bit old to be Rose's classmate. Thought you ought to know." I heard a ding in the background. "Gotta run, Stone, order's up." He was gone before I could thank him.

Pat had called too. It was a while before Greenberg was due back at the office, and I was too antsy to just sit. I grabbed my hat and walked down to his bar. Nine in the morning is long before Pat opens, but that doesn't mean he's not there working. I tapped on the window, and he waved from behind the bar. A moment later, he unlocked the door and latched it again behind me.

"Get my note, Casey?"

"Yeah, and I had a minute and smelled your coffee."

He laughed and reached for the pot as I slid onto a barstool. He set a cup in front of me, filled it, and topped off his. He leaned on the bar and asked, "How's it going with Rose's case?"

"Making some progress. Why?"

"Casey, I don't know what it's about, and I don't want to, but in the last couple of days, some woman has been nosing around asking about you, what kind of cases you handle, and particularly wondering if you could help locate missing persons. She looked real business-like. She was early to mid 40's, medium height, well dressed."

"Not the kind of gal that's usually hunting me."

"She had a real nice emerald ring on her right pinky, and she's left-handed, because I saw her writing a note before she left. When she came in, she told me she was in a hurry, that she had a strict lunch hour."

"Some people do, you know."

"It smelled funny 'cause you're in the book and just a block away. She could have called you or gone by your office as easy as come by here. Nobody mentioned Rose by name, but the woman was fishing. You might want to tell Rose. She hasn't been back in since I sent her your way."

"Thanks Pat. Sounds like the same broad that visited Manny's. You know I got shot at. Did you hear about the CPA getting shot yesterday a couple of blocks from here?" He nodded. "That wasn't coincidence. He was connected to the case, and I had just seen him the day before. I warned him to be careful, but the bad guys are playing rough. Nobody saw anything, but two goons are working together. One is big and pasty-faced and probably has his nose taped, 'cause I busted it two days ago. The other one is tall and thin and wears a white suit. Both of them carry pistols.

I'll get 'em, but until then, everybody around me has to be cautious."

"Casey, I've got three of these under the bar." He reached down and laid a billy-club down on the bar with a solid thump. "I haven't run a bar for twenty-five years without knowing how to use one. I've also got a sawed-off right under the cashbox. Only had to use it once. Some doped-up punk tried to rob me in broad daylight. At two feet, it made a hell of a mess of him, but the cops knew me and the investigation was short. They called it self-defense and didn't do anything about the shotgun except to say, "Keep it loaded.""

I drained my cup. Pat waved off my nickel for the coffee, and I headed back to the office.

Chiquita was answering the phone as I walked in. "Oh, here he is right now, Mr. Greenberg." I grabbed my desk phone and answered.

"Mr. Stone, when did you last talk to Miss Kelly?"

"Must have been day before yesterday. Why?"

"I have just returned from a private chambers conference with the Family Court Judge that handled her child's adoption sixteen years ago. I conferred with Miss Kelly and prepared a petition to unseal the records based on her affidavit concerning her underage status, supported by a certified copy of her own birth certificate. No other parties were referred to in the petition except The Home.

"I don't ordinarily do family law myself," Greenberg continued, "but the Judge and I go back to law school days at Columbia, so my credibility is not an issue. He is very concerned about the allegations we've made about questionable practices at The Home, and the legal disposition of custody of these vulnerable children.

"Mr. Stone, our conference was completely confidential. Not even the Judge's secretary knows the subject matter, a situation she found highly irritating, as she has been with the Judge at least twenty years and considers herself the power behind the throne. A rather severe looking lady—very professional, no wedding ring—her work is her life, I suppose. I had to threaten to call His Honor at home, before she relented and made the appointment without a full disclosure of the facts. Of course, the Judge will pull the file to review and Miss Gatekeeper will then know who's involved. The Judge told me to come back at 8:30 tomorrow."

"Mr. Greenberg, you are a hell of an advocate! How can I help?"

"This whole matter is rather delicate considering who might be involved, the size of the trust fund, and my own ethical situation. I represent the deceased and the trust he established. Its terms are clear: his daughter is the primary beneficiary if she is living and can be found. I am directed to exert all reasonable efforts to determine those facts. But there is, of course, the alternate beneficiary if the daughter cannot be located within thirty days, or is deceased. I have an ethical obligation to both. The Court has an obligation of fairness, which will eventually require a legal notice to the alternate beneficiary and all parties involved in the original proceedings sixteen years ago.

"Stone, we need our facts as firmly established as possible before that hearing occurs. I cannot change the thirty-day period in the trust. I can only seek expedited court proceedings. I am relying on you, sir, for the facts, and quickly."

"Counselor, we are in a chicken-or-the-egg spot here. A lot of the necessary facts are in that sealed court file. They would point me in the right direction to locate the girl. But if I hear you right, when that file is opened, everybody will get those facts at the same time, including Joey Catalano, as well as the original parties, which probably includes Mr. Menaphy, who may well have that girl locked up on his property."

"You are exactly correct, Mr. Stone. Not an enviable position for any of us, but unavoidable, I fear."

I hung up the phone with a sinking heart. There could be a hearing in a few days. Joey would show up with the best legal eagles mob money could buy. Menaphy would show up with even better legal talent. Rose would show up with Greenberg and me and a lot of hollow allegations if I couldn't produce anything more than my suspicions. We were going to go down in flames if I couldn't get at those Home records—and fast.

Chapter 12

"Chiquita, come in, please." As she entered, I waved her to the seat in front of my desk. "Chick, we're in a bind." I told her what Greenberg said about the urgent need of facts quickly, and my conclusion that our only hope was to get a look at the files at The Home. "Does your aunt still work there?"

She said, "Yes, but Tia really works for a cleaning service that goes in on Friday evenings for about three hours to do the heavy-duty work. They are usually there about 6:00 PM to 9:00 PM."

"Do you think you could get on the crew and get a look at those files? It ought to be me, but we're hurting for time, and I can't figure out how to get in there other than an outright break-in."

"Boss, I put myself through PI school working nights on cleaning crews. I know what to do, but I don't know if I can get on the staff. I probably still have some good references, but I need to talk to my aunt." She left for her desk, and I was left with worries about a 16-year-old girl who might be a sex slave, but didn't know that she was also a murder target.

I needed to take my mind off the case for a while, and I was overdue to clean up some of the backlog on my desk. I dictated a report to a wife whose husband ran off with his secretary. I tracked them to Atlantic City posing as newlyweds and had the photos to prove it.

A white Cadillac had disappeared from Manhattan with twelve payments owing and turned up black, with out-of-state plates, in Brooklyn.

A guy in SoHo passed four bad checks. He had a little insurance business, and a big business betting on the horses. A few bad bets and suddenly his checks were looking like the basketballs at a Harlem Globetrotters' game. I showed up at his office and told him he was lucky his checks were bouncing rather than his bookie accounts because I'd give him two weeks to make good, and I wasn't going to break his legs. What I was going to do was make a report to his parent insurance company, the Department of Insurance, and his wife. It was the last threat that made him ill. He cleared all of his checks with three days to spare.

Chiquita came strutting back to my desk. "I'm in for this Friday. I still have my papers from schooldays. Tia and I talked and made up the story that she needed off because her boyfriend was taking her to visit his family in Philadelphia, but she could have her niece fill in. Tia usually does the offices anyway, so it should work. I'm meeting her tonight to get the layout and talk about where the records are kept and what kind of security there is. The only person who has office keys is the foreman on the crew. She unlocks the doors as they need them."

Friday was two days off. We spent the rest of the day talking about what to look for, where it might be in the records, and practicing her lock picking. We'd have a problem if there were combination locks, even with her stethoscope. But she was slick with the lock picks. She could get in our file cabinet in about a minute when we started, and about twenty seconds when we finished. She was practicing on the desk locks and my door lock when I left for lunch.

I picked up a foot-long hoagie and headed for my apartment. I stuck my head in the Super's apartment, and before I could ask, he said, "It's been as quiet as a church the day after Easter." I tossed him a pack of Camels with a smile and my thanks.

Alias Baby Girl

Suzie opened the door as soon as she heard my voice. As we ate, I confirmed that it was today, Wednesday, when the hard-faced man visited Joey for the weekly pick-up. "Yes, he always come at 5:30. He never speak. He just walk back, stay ten minutes, and leave. He have a briefcase. Joey alway send Sam and Felix away for about an hour so they never there when the man comes."

"Who did Uncle Chen get for your replacement?"

"A new girl—daughter of a friend of his."

"Does she know anything about Joey?"

"Uncle tell her not to see anybody or anything back there."

Joey was already on my tail. I'd been shot at, Simon had been killed, and they wrote me a message on his desk pad. I saw a way to hit back where it would really hurt Joey and help Rose.

At ten minutes until 5:00, I was window-shopping across from Chen's Cleaners. Inside a Macy's bag, I had a briefcase. Sam and Felix strolled out and headed north a couple of minutes after 5:00. As soon as they were out of sight, I dumped the bag, crossed the street holding my briefcase, and walked to Joey's door without a glance toward the counter girl. As soon as I was behind the rack of clothes, I tied my handkerchief across my face just like a cowboy bandit. I tried the doorknob. It was locked, but the door wasn't pulled completely shut. I drew Betsy, pushed the safety off, and pushed the door open.

Joey was kneeling in front of his open wall safe. He whirled around and jumped for his desk drawer when he saw the mask. I got there first and slammed it shut on his hand. As he started to yowl, I brought the .45 down as hard as I could on the side of his head. It made a satisfying sound—sort of like Mickey Mantle slapping a homerun in the bottom of the ninth to win the game. I kicked his legs out of the way and cleaned out the safe, cash and paper filling my briefcase. I stuffed my handkerchief back in my pocket and left, pulling the door closed behind me.

I caught the Lexington Avenue subway south and was halfway to the Village before I quit chuckling to myself. I

57

enjoyed the thought of Joey with a splitting headache and an empty safe dealing with the hard-faced man who doubtless had called his boss as soon as Joey came up short. I laughed again at the chewing out that Sam and Felix would get for failing to protect mob property.

When I got to the office, it was locked, but Chick had left a note that she was down to fifteen seconds to pop my file cabinet lock, and she'd see me in the morning. I locked both doors to my office and emptied the briefcase on my desk.

The cash was easy. It was already counted into $1,000 packets held by rubber bands. There were eleven packets, but one had a note stuck under the rubber band that said $981.00. I put all of it into a cloth bank bag I kept as a souvenir from a prior case and locked it in my safe.

The paperwork was betting tickets that probably would prove to be a worse loss for Joey than the cash. A lot of regulars would have enough clout to demand payment in amounts Joey couldn't disprove and couldn't pay without the boys upstate funding his piggybank. The big boys were expecting deposits into their coffers, not withdrawals by a two-bit hood who couldn't handle his own security. Worse for him, they would figure he sent his men away so he could skim the weekly take without witnesses. There was going to be a lot of unhappiness for Joey in the next few days. I laughed out loud and put them in the safe as well and locked it.

Rose answered the phone with a slurred hello. Glen Miller's Band played low in the background. "Am I interrupting, Rose?"

"No, Big Boy, I'm just dancing solo, thinking about all the things I've missed in my life and crying about Angel." I was sorry I called.

"Look, Babe, no need to be blue. Things are moving in the right direction. The next few days are going to be crucial, and you need to be at your best. I've talked with Lawyer Greenberg; he's meeting with the Judge in the morning. There could be an emergency hearing anytime, and you would need to testify. To stand a chance, you'll have to knock 'em dead, just like you did the first time you walked in my office. Now, be a good girl and put yourself to bed."

She was humming with the record. "Won't you come over and tuck me in?"

"No, Baby, not tonight. I'm working on your case and have to meet someone." I was lying, but not entirely, as I was going to ask Suzie some more questions about Joey's operation.

I could still hear Glen Miller, but not Rose. "Rose, are you still there?"

"Still here, Casey," she said dreamily. "Are you sure you can't come over?"

"Listen, Rose," I said sharply. "Turn that record player off." The receiver clattered on the table and in a minute the music ended in a loud scratch—one Glen Miller record headed for the trash bin. In a few seconds, the receiver clattered again, and I heard her breathing.

"Rose, can you hear me?"

"Yes, lover."

"Rose, shut up and listen. I called to tell you to be careful. One of the people I talked to about you was shot and killed yesterday. I'm sure it was Joey's goons. You've got to be careful. Are you listening?"

When she answered, she was still drunk, but she was thinking. "Casey, what should I do?"

"Make sure your door is locked and when you go out, you pay close attention to everybody on the sidewalk and every car on the street. Remember, they shot at me on Houston Street at 9:30 in the morning. Make sure your apartment superintendent knows you are being harassed and to watch traffic in and out of your building really close. Got it?"

"Got it, Casey." Her tone was frightened now. "I wish you were here."

Chapter 13

I got up long before Suzie was awake and caught breakfast on the way to the office. I pulled the betting records out of the safe and studied them, trying to get a handle on how much dough was involved. I couldn't concentrate. I kept thinking about Greenberg meeting with the Judge. Time crept slowly. I went down to the corner newsstand and got a paper from Jimmy and tried to read the news. Even the baseball scores didn't hold my attention. Finally, it was late enough for Greenberg's office to open. I called, and Maureen noted that I was the first caller of the day.

"Is he in yet? I know he had a chambers conference again this morning."

"No, he's not in yet, Mr. Early Bird. Even if the judge was prompt and even if the conference was only five minutes, he hasn't had time to get back. Besides, he told me it might be lengthy."

"Sorry, Maureen. I'm really antsy about this case." I backed up and re-started. "Are you wearing one of those really fine suits again?"

"Now, that's more like it," she purred. "I just put on the coffee. Why don't you come up and have some and wait for Mr. Greenberg here. Then you can check out the suit for yourself."

It was an irresistible offer. I left a note for Chick and hailed a cab going north on Park Avenue. Seven minutes later, I tipped him and headed for the fancy elevators. As I opened the great oaken door, Maureen looked up over the counter and said, "My, you're fast."

"Some people have said so, but when a woman says she just put on the coffee and a fancy suit for me, I don't want to waste a moment. And yes, it is really a fine outfit." I hung my hat on the coat rack and sat on the sofa.

She laughed as she headed down the hall for the coffee. I knew the drill. She paused, looked over her shoulder, and laughed again as she ducked into the kitchen. Coming back she looked even better. No scarf at the throat today, and when she set my cup down, her cups almost overflowed.

She stood and slowly turned around grinning the whole time. There was no part of her that wasn't luscious. "Well," she said teasingly. "Do I pass inspection?"

"It's a good thing I have a strong heart, Maureen. Too much of you is a great thing. Did you have to pass a screen test to get this job?"

"No, Silly Boy. But I did dress right for the interview."

"Now that's an interview I'd like to conduct."

"And it's one I would like to come to."

"I couldn't pay you what you're worth."

"You might not have to. There are always fringe benefits to consider."

"If Chiquita ever leaves me, you'll be the first to know."

"Oh," she pouted. "The other woman always gets there first. It's OK though. I believe that saying that a man wants to be a woman's first lover, but a woman wants to be a man's last."

I let that roll around my mind for a moment, and then said, "Maureen, you're special. I wish we had met at a different time. But this is the wrong time, even if we are the right people."

She started to say something when the switchboard buzzed, and the moment passed. Things got busy for her, and I flipped through last month's Esquire, killing time, not really reading.

At last, a buzz and Maureen said, "He's here in the reception room. Yes, sir, I'll bring him right back." As we walked briskly toward Mr. Greenberg's office, she whispered, "He seems really excited." She knocked at his door, and he opened it himself.

"Thanks, Maureen. Come in Mr. Stone." He was excited. He didn't sit, but paced back and forth as he gave me the news.

"You, sir...well, we...have opened Pandora's box. When I arrived at the judge's office, his secretary was even less cordial than before, but ushered me into his chamber without delay. The judge was agitated. After looking at our file yesterday, he sent the clerk to the archives and pulled every file involving The Home for the last 20 years. He said there are at least 25 that appear to be like ours—underage mothers signing under duress."

"Mr. Stone, he was beside himself at the enormity of hurt and injustice those files might represent."

"'*And to think,*' the judge told me, '*that this court, established to do justice and equity, may have aided and abetted these wrongs. David,*' he said, '*I'm setting your petition for a hearing a week from Friday, the minimal time for proper notice to the necessary parties. I'm clearing my entire docket and this case will be first. If your Miss Kelly testifies like her affidavit, I will bring the full weight of the law upon these miscreants. If you need subpoenas, you shall have them. If you need injunctions, you shall have them. I will not have this court misused as a bludgeon on the innocent. David, you bring me a case that will stand review, and I will blow this thing...*'"

"Stone," he became quite speechless. "I thanked him, excused myself, and almost ran back here. Stone, we've got work to do. Those subpoenas sound good, but even if we sent them today for the records at The Home on Rose's case, they will claim they can't be found due to their age. By the time we drag them to court, all the evidence will have been destroyed...'proper disposition of out-of-date records,' or some such tripe. Stone, I've got to have something to wave at the judge so we know where the trail is to that baby girl."

Alias Baby Girl

"Teenager now, Mr. Lawyer, and if she's anything like her mother, a knockout. I've got a strong lead, but I won't know how it will pan out for a couple of days."

Chapter 14

I knew Greenberg would not use any illegal evidence. But what he didn't know wouldn't hurt him. So, I didn't mention Chiquita's proposed foray into the nooks and crannies of The Home. I said my goodbyes to him and Maureen and headed back downtown.

The problem that kept buzzing around my head like an annoying fly was Angel's predicament. Assuming Menaphy was the person who got her 16 years ago, and assuming she was a resident in the Menaphy estate, once the legal dam broke, he or Joey would have plenty of time to arrange an accident or some other story to explain her disappearance. I grimaced at the irony of it: Joey Catalano and Joseph K. Menaphy would probably loathe each other, but fate had led them to a common goal—eliminating Angel—and I had to find a way to save her.

I caught a cab back to my office. Chiquita was there, practicing lock picking. She gave me a glance and a nod and kept at it. I looked at her for a moment and thought that I had never seen a cleaning lady that looked so good. No wonder she took up judo.

I sat at my desk, grabbed the phone, and called my apartment, let it ring twice, hung up, and then redialed. Suzie picked up with a quiet, "Yes."

"How's my China doll this morning?"

"Casey, I need to get out. I miss my work, my people, shopping for food, fresh air. I have your flat as clean as it can get."

"Suzie, I didn't bring you there to work, or to put up with my foul moods. It's just the safest place I know, and it won't be for much longer. Trust me. Things are moving fast now, and maybe Joey will go away and things will be OK. Suzie, I'm going to bring you a little present tonight." By the time she begged to know, and I teased her leaving it a mystery, she felt better.

I had seen a single pearl in a white gold setting on a delicate rope necklace at the jewelers down the street that always worked on my watch. It would be perfect for Suzie.

I took a deep breath and called Rose's work. A twangy Jersey woman answered and said to hold the line after I told her who I was. Rose was all business when she answered, until she heard my voice. "Casey, did I act the fool last night?"

"No, Rosie, you acted like you were overdue for a break. How do you feel?"

"Head not so good, but I'm here. A girl's gotta work, if a girl's gonna eat."

"See if this helps the head. Greenberg got a hearing Friday after next to unseal the records and the judge as much as told him if you make as good a witness as your affidavit, it's a done deal." After a few seconds, I heard the sniffles. "Casey, I don't know how to thank you."

"Rosie, it's not just me. It's you, Chiquita, Greenberg, Captain Butler, and me, all aiming to do right by that girl. But we aren't home free. Even if the file is unsealed, we still got to find her, but this is a good first step."

Next call was to Steve Butler. When he heard my voice, he said, "Same place we met last time," and hung up. Uh-oh, problems at the office. Didn't use my name, or even say the place we were meeting.

I told Chiquita I was headed to Queenie's for an early lunch and walked out of the office with a bit of foreboding.

Robert W. Godwin

Things were normal at Queenie's. I waved at her and headed for an empty booth at the back. She met me with two frosted beers. What a great place.

"Your pal coming?"

I grunted at her, frosted mug at my lips.

"Roast beef sandwich with fries is today's lunch special."

I grunted again and held up two fingers, before I put my glass down.

"Nice manners, PI," she said laughing her way back to the bar.

Ben Franklin was right:beer is proof that God loves us and wants us to be happy. I headed to the restroom and Steve was in the booth when I got back. He didn't wait for me to get settled before he leaned forward and said intently, "Casey, you've got a problem."

"I got a bunch of problems. Which one are you talking about?"

"You've got a leak. I got an anonymous call not 10 minutes before you rang me. I hear the lawyer got an expedited hearing on his petition to unseal the records. It's set Friday week at 9:00 AM before Judge Hubert McCain, and if you bust this one, there are 25 more coming down the pike. Subpoenas will be issued wherever your attorney wants."

"Damn!" I slapped the table so hard the glasses jumped. "Steve, Greenberg almost ran from the judge's chambers to tell me. It was just the two of them. I told Rose and that's it. That's it! I haven't even told Chiquita yet."

I sat there stunned. They had a 36-hour lead on us. Even if Chiquita's gig went perfectly, she was looking for those records a day and a half late. I pounded the table again, and then buried my head in my hands.

Food arrived and mine sat there untouched. Queenie looked at me, then at Steve, and raised an eyebrow. Steve just shook her off. When Steve had finished his sandwich and was drowning his fries in ketchup, he said, "There's another bit of news from the Upper East Side Precinct. They aren't officially involved, because there's been no report, but the word on the street is somebody knocked Joey

66

Catalano in the head and emptied his safe. We do know he visited Mt. Sinai Hospital ER and refused admission, although he had a severe concussion. The nurse's notes say, 'Patient reports he fell against desk,' but the wound was in a funny location on his skull for that. He got a shaved spot, ten stitches, and some pain pills. Two fellows drove him off when he was released against medical advice."

I started on my sandwich and listened silently. When he was done, I asked between bites, "What do you figure was in the safe?"

Steve looked thoughtful for a few fries, and then replied, "cash of course, records, tout slips, stuff on bets. I'd love for our accountants to have a look at something like that."

"Steve, you know I've spent some time up there in the last few days. I'll spread the word that there would be some mighty grateful cops if something like that were mailed to your office in a plain brown wrapper marked 'Attention: Captain Butler.' A cop would remember a favor like that for a long time, I bet."

Steve was staring at me with a fry halfway to his mouth. I stuffed the last bite of my sandwich in my mouth and avoided his eyes. After a moment or two, he finished the fry and said carefully, "A favor like that would go a long way towards smoothing over some misunderstandings the department has had with some irritating individuals in our fair city. NYPD strives for community cooperation and goodwill." His voice trailed off.

"Those words are great speech material, Steve. Do you think they'd actually deliver if such a thing were to happen? You know, if they knew who to thank?"

"If I was involved, Casey, they wouldn't get the benefit of the favor if they weren't going to reciprocate. One hand washes the other, in my book."

"I never doubted it for a minute, Steve. Right now, my big concern is the leak. Who could it be?"

Chapter 15

Steve downed the last of his beer and called for the check. While they were figuring it, he leaned back, replaying the case. "It was a man, indeterminate age, muffled voice, possible Italian accent, street noise in the background—probably using a phone booth, spoke hurriedly, and didn't wait for an answer before hanging up. Knew to call me, so he knew of my connection to you and that you'd hear it pronto. You're chasing two leads: Joey Catalano—there's an Italian connection; and the adoptive person who may be Menaphy—an Irish connection. If you knew where the leak started, you'd probably be able to chase down our caller. He's got something to lose or he would have just called you or at least identified himself. The station house has ears too, so I didn't give any facts when I called you."

Steve thought in checklists. It was why he was such a good cop and why it helped me to talk a case through with him. He paid the tab and we both left mulling over the questions.

I took the "Out to Lunch" sign off my office door, unlocked it and immediately called Greenberg. He was as stunned as I was to hear of the leak. "But no one knows, except the Judge, me, you, Rose."

"Think, Mr. Greenberg, did you tell anybody in your office?"

"No, you were here when I arrived, and I met directly with you."

"Did you talk to anyone at the Courthouse?"

"No. As I told you, the Judge was agitated, and I was so eager to get back that I almost ran over his secretary." He paused, then thinking out loud said, "Of course, she relayed the request for files...and she will handle his docket setting...and send the notices..."

It clicked. I interrupted. "David, tell me again what she looks like."

"Well, late 30s...early 40s. Not unattractive, always well dressed, very professional, no wedding ring."

"Any other jewelry?"

"Why yes, an extraordinary emerald ring surrounded by diamonds. A beautiful piece and quite expensive, I would judge."

"Do you know her name?"

"Her desk plate says Maria Fregossi," he said spelling the last name.

"David, we may have our leak. She's the only one who knew about the hearing as early as we did." I told him of the woman nosing around Rose's old neighborhood and mine. "Who would know her background?"

"Well, outside of the Judge himself, I don't know. We have a couple of family law specialists in the firm who regularly appear in that court. I'll check with them and get back to you."

As I hung up, the office door swung open and Chiquita waltzed in with a flourish and a shopping bag. "Look what I found," she said, pulling out a beautiful silk blouse with a brilliant red orchid print. "It matches my favorite shade of lipstick, see?" She held it up to her chest and whirled around the room, happy as a schoolgirl at Christmas.

"Really nice, Chick. I can hardly wait to see you in it." It was truer than I wanted to admit. I pushed the memory of the taste of her lipstick from my mind, gently rubbed my sore ribs and said, "We have a leak in the case." I briefed her about the hearing, the leak, and confessed, "I'm worried the bad guys are getting ahead of us. But the leak came from the other side, and we think it started with the Judge's secretary, Maria Fregossi."

Robert W. Godwin

"And Chick, this puts even more pressure on us to get information tomorrow night when you work that cleaning crew."

She nodded silently, returned the blouse to the bag, and broke out her lock picking kit.

I called Manny. Business was slow, and he could talk.

"Manny, that woman nosing around the deli might be named Fregossi. Ever hear that name?"

"Hear it?! There must be a hundred of them in the neighborhood. What's it about?"

I told him, and I could see him rubbing his chin, rolling that over in his mind. "There must be a dozen Maria's. Most have stayed in family businesses or stuck to raising kids. Yours is unmarried and nobody here recognized her, but she did know the neighborhood..."

I asked him to think about it and let me know if anything turned up, and dialed Rose.

"Rose, you ever heard of a Maria Fregossi?"

"Sure, Casey, sister of my first boyfriend, Marcello. We had a mutual crush in sixth grade. He was 13, and I was 12. I'll never forget..."

"OK, OK. Was she older or younger than him?"

"Maybe five years older. Why?"

I told her.

"Geez, Casey, Marc and I stayed friends through high school. He was always a sweet guy, but his sister was snooty and mean. He said it was because she was jealous of me being pretty. I was glad when she moved to the Bronx with some cousins."

"What happened to him?"

"I lost track, but the last I heard he still lived in the old neighborhood. He didn't go into the family restaurant. He was a genius with figures and was working after school for the local bookie while he was still in grammar school."

"Rose, you know what I said about being careful—that goes double now. Somebody is well informed enough to know you, that I'm working for you, and why I visited Joey and roughed up one of his goons. They must know that Captain Butler and I were both at Simon's office after he got

70

shot and what the Judge is doing. When the guy called, he wouldn't identify himself, but he was willing to take a chance to let us know there was a leak."

"OK, Casey, I'll be careful. Got to get back to work." After we hung up, I sat there, elbows on the desk, head in hands, thinking how to break this deadlock. We'd gone from a couple of rounds ahead to a couple of rounds behind in a heavyweight fight we had to win, and it made me ill.

I thought about the cash and records I took from Joey's safe. I yelled for Chiquita in the front office. "Have we got some plain brown wrapping paper?" She came to the door with lock picks in her hand.

"Sure, why?"

"I've got something I have to send to Captain Butler anonymously."

"What is it?"

"Babe, it is better that you don't know, so if you get asked you can answer honestly. I'll tell you all about it later."

She started to object, thought about it, then turned back to the front office and reappeared with a thirty inch roll of plain brown paper and a roll of cellophane tape. "I guess you'll want to wrap it, so I don't see anything either."

"That's why I hired you, girl. You're smart as well as pretty." She stuck out her tongue and pulled the door shut behind her. It didn't take ten minutes to wrap it up and write on the front, "CAPT. BUTLER PERSONAL". I wrote with my left hand and was satisfied it didn't look like me.

I opened the door, told Chiquita I'd be back in about a half an hour and took the stairs with the package under my arm. I stopped at the newsstand on the next block. "Hey, Jimmy. When is that kid that makes deliveries for you going to show up?"

"After school, Casey. Any time now."

"Would you mind if he dropped this package off for me at the precinct with the evening papers?"

"Any message?"

"No, no, Jimmy! Don't tell him anything and if he asks, just tell him you're doing a favor for a customer, but don't use my name. OK? Here, give him a buck."

"Sure, Casey. I get it. Glad to help."

"I owe you one, Jimmy, and I'll take a paper myself."

I paid my dime and headed for the jeweler's. The necklace was still in the window, glowing on a black velvet background. Suzie would love it. I paid the clerk and had her gift wrap it and stuck it in my coat pocket. I waved to the owner as he peered over his watchmaker's bench at the rear, and left feeling better than I had in a while.

The package would get to Steve maybe an hour before his shift ended, and I expected a call right before he left for the day. I caught myself whistling a little as I headed back to the office.

Chapter 16

I knew it was bad when I swung open the door. Chiquita was pale, and she'd been crying.

"Your building supervisor just called and said it was an emergency."

I dropped the paper, turned and ran down the stairs, down the street and finally to my building. There were two cops out front stringing crime tape. The younger one tried to stop me, but the older one recognized me and waved me through. It wouldn't have mattered. I was full speed up the steps and to the Super's apartment. His door was open, and I saw a detective seated in one of his chairs, taking his statement. Luther looked up, holding a bloody rag to his head. "Awww, Casey, I'm so sorry! There were two of them, and they hit me while I was taking the trash out ...."

I didn't wait for him to finish, but bounded up the stairs to my floor. The broken door was blocked by Steve talking to another cop. As soon as he saw me, he held up his hand and said, "Casey, you don't want to see this." I knew I didn't, but I had to, and pushed by him into my living room and elbowed the crime photographer aside.

Suzie was lying on the sofa, more beautiful than ever, except for the red blotch on the bathrobe over her heart. Time froze. I couldn't breathe. I couldn't take my eyes off her. couldn't talk. I reached out and stroked her cheek, which was still warm. With a sudden catch in my throat, I bent over, hands on either side of her face, and kissed her lips.

Steve put his arm around my shoulders, gently pulling me toward the kitchen table. "Come in here, Casey, and let the boys do their job."

We sat. He asked questions. I numbly gave answers. He took notes, the photographer took pictures, and the medical examiner took the body to the morgue.

At last Steve stood up and looked at me a long time before speaking. Casey, you're not in shape to decide anything right now. It's a police matter, and you know I'll work it hard. I know the background. I know where to look. It's the same guys that shot the CPA. I'll build a case that the greenest DA could convict on. But it'll take some time. The only thing that could screw it up is you going off on a tear. Understand?"

I heard it all. I knew he was right. I couldn't answer because of the lump in my throat. I nodded silently at him.

"You ought to spend a couple of days with your aunt down at Barnegat. Walk the beach. Eat some home-cooked food. Breathe some fresh air. Give yourself a break. You'll be a lot more use to Rose and her kid if you do." I nodded again, hoping he'd get the hell out before I broke down completely. He stood there a second longer and said softly, "Hang in there pal," patted my shoulder and left.

I took in a long shuddering breath, trying to steady myself and caught a faint whiff of jasmine. My ears heard the wail of anguish, pain and frustration long before my mind recognized it was mine. I was spinning in a black swirl of grief and remorse at my loss and my failure to protect Suzie when I gradually became aware of someone calling my name over and over.

"Casey, Casey. Look at me, Casey. It's Chiquita. It's me, Boss."

I saw her dimly through the haze of my tears and grief coming toward me with arms spread wide. She wrapped them around me, drawing my head to her, rocking gently back and forth, crooning something Spanish, as I wept and cursed and moaned until exhaustion overtook me.

I woke to an obnoxious deejay announcing it was seven o'clock and going to be a great Friday. It wasn't going to be great. I felt drained, sour, and empty. Suzie was dead. Rose's case was in jeopardy. I was the lousiest PI in the state.

I sat up in my bed still in yesterday's clothes except for the coat and tie hanging on the bedside chair. Then I remembered Chiquita with a mix of embarrassment and gratitude. I stumbled to the door and saw her on the living room floor wrapped in a blanket on a pallet made of a chair pad and two sofa pads. The third sofa pad was nowhere to be seen, I realized with relief. She had braced the door with a kitchen chair, which held it shut despite the broken frame and lock. I tiptoed past her and started the percolator.

I quietly showered, dressed, and when I went back for coffee, she was sitting on the chair, pads replaced, trying to fluff her hair.

"Don't look at me like this, Boss," she pleaded in a little girl voice.

I poured two cups and carried them to the table beside her and set them down. She turned away, trying to hide her face. I knelt in front of her and gently took her face in my hands, turning it till we were eye to eye. "Chiquita, a guy couldn't have a better friend. You'll always be beautiful to me, no matter what." Tears welled in her eyes and rolled down the smudged mascara.

"This is Friday...show time tonight for you. But Chiquita, you don't have to do it. These guys are smart and they're really playing rough—first the CPA, now Suzie right here. They knew where to look, and they got past Luther. There's no question they know about you. There's no shame in deciding not to go."

"Casey Stone!" The hands were on the hips. "Do I look yellow to you? Do you think I'm chicken? Have you ever known me to back down from a fight?" Smudged mascara or no, the eyes were flashing. "Three brothers step out of my way. Not go? Not go?! I may not care about your Rosie, but I care a lot about that kid!"

Robert W. Godwin

I looked at her for a moment: moldering eyes, lips pressed together, shiny black hair framing her face. I knew better than to laugh. "Stupid of me to suggest it, Babe. I should have known better. If you want to take the day off, it's OK, because tonight, as soon as you get back from The Home, I want to look at anything you found."

"Maybe I will lay out, Boss. I was up pretty late cleaning, but I couldn't save the sofa pad..." The scene flashed through my mind, and I quivered with rage. This was war and from now on, I intended for all the casualties to be on the other side.

"It's OK. Here's a ten spot. We'll send you home in a cab now and tonight you call the cab and have him waiting to come back here. You need to be careful."

After a quick session in front of the mirror, she gathered her things, and I walked her out to the street and watched until she was safely in the cab. I called down to Luther and told him I was dumping the sofa and wanted the door fixed as quickly as possible. He said he already had the new door delivered and would be up shortly. He started to apologize again, but I cut him off with, "Not your fault, Luther, not your fault. How's the head?" He said he'd live and he'd take the sofa out when he was done with the door.

I sat with the pot of coffee at the kitchen table trying not to think. It was on my third refill that I noticed my cup—my favorite cup—was sparkling clean. As the tears started, I heard Luther and his helper headed for the door. I jumped up and pretended to wash a couple of dishes and yelled at them to come on in. I told him I had to run some errands, and I'd check with him for the new key when I got back. I grabbed my hat and coat and took the stairs. As I got outside and took a deep breath to steady my nerves, I felt the crinkle in my coat pocket—the gift-wrapped necklace.

I bent over the railing and gripped it with both hands, fighting with all my might not to scream or collapse sobbing on the landing or run wildly down the street. This was crazy. I always ruled my emotions, not the other way around. I was going to kill the bastards who did this to her,

76

not be swept along by tears and tissues like some high school girl.

I don't know how much time passed, but I realized both hands were clamped like claws on the railing, and I was gasping for breath. I forced my hands off the rail, stuck them in my pockets and headed for Pat's.

He glanced up before I rapped on the window and opened the door.

"Jesus, what the hell is the matter with you?"

My story started over a cup of coffee and ended over a jigger of whisky. It's true: a friend in need is a friend in deed. All Pat did was listen, pour, and finally toast her memory with me. It was enough.

"Pat, what would you do in my shoes?"

"Kill the bastards."

"Exactly what I intend to do."

"Of course, you have to kill the right bastards."

"Steve told me to lay off, he'd get 'em."

"And he will, Casey. But it won't be the same, because he's got to hand them over to the courts."

"And they'll cop a plea, the mob will keep them on the payroll while they're doing time, and they'll be out in five years with a nice little nest egg. Damn it, Pat!"

"I agree, Casey. Too good for them. Your way is better. But you've got to be careful or you'll end up in the clink instead of them. Tell you the truth, maybe you'd better think about it some more and make sure you know what you're doing."

I thanked him, and fortified with five jiggers of Irish whisky headed back to the jeweler's where I returned the necklace for a full refund and got a promise from him not to display it in the window again. I didn't think I could stand to see it.

I picked up a paper from Jimmy, who said his delivery boy had given the package to Captain Butler personally at his office. The Captain had taken it, looked at it, and asked where it came from. The boy didn't know and got a fifty cent tip and left.

Robert W. Godwin

When I got to the office, I found five pieces of mail on the floor inside the door behind the mail slot.

Chapter 17

I left the "Closed" sign on the office door as I shut it behind me. I gathered the mail and laid it on my desk with the newspaper and unfolded it. Nothing much on the front page. On page eight, I saw it.

Hit and Run Kills Judge

> Well-known and respected Family Court Judge Hubert McNair died last night at New York Hospital Emergency Room where he was taken by ambulance after being hit by an automobile near his apartment. Witnesses at the scene said the judge was crossing West 50th Street at Ninth Avenue with the traffic light when a black Ford ran the red light and failed to stop after hitting the victim. No further information was available at press time.

Dumbstruck, I read and reread the article. I dialed Steve. When he picked up, I asked, "Have you seen the morning paper?"

"No, Casey, I haven't, but we kept everything quiet about your place."

"Steve, they got our judge!"

"What?!" I heard the rustle of paper.

"It's on page eight. Will you check with that precinct and fill me in? I'm at the office."

Over the sound of turning pages, he said, "I guess you aren't going to Barnegat, huh?"

"You got it. I'm going to check with Greenberg and see what happens now with Rose's case. I'll get back with you. I've got to call Rose." I paused before I continued. "Steve, thanks for being there yesterday."

He pretended not to hear. "Hey, before you rush off, I got an anonymous package yesterday right before the beat cop called in about your place."

"Oh?"

"I barely had a chance to open it. It held about eleven thousand dollars cash and a bunch of records that look like a bookie operation and maybe the take on a stable of girls."

"No joke!"

"You must really have some connections, Casey. We only had that conversation two days ago."

"Well, Captain Butler, until you find the real public spirited citizen, direct all that gratitude to me, OK? I think that cash will make a fine contribution to The Policemen's Benevolent Fund, don't you?"

He hung up laughing. My spirits quickly sank back to a dark and murky blue, but I had no time to mope and dialed again. Befitting a high tone major law firm, Maureen answered on the first ring.

"It's Casey Stone. Is David in?"

"My, aren't we brusque today?"

"Sorry, Babe. This is an emergency. Well?"

"He is, but he's with a client."

"Slip him a note. I'm on the way and have to see him."

I hung up and was writing Chiquita a note in case she came by, when I remembered the mail. I recognized the utility bill, the rent statement, and the renewal notice on my PI license. The ad for office space in a new building in SoHo went into the trash. The last envelope had no return address. The address was typed and it was postmarked a little after midnight at the Central Post Office at 33rd Street and Eighth Avenue, which is open around the clock. I stuck it in my pocket, grabbed the paper, and caught a cab to midtown to see Greenberg.

I was getting too familiar with those massive oak doors and gilt lettering. Maureen was on the phone and waved me to a seat. When she hung up, she headed for the coffee without a word and returned with a cup. I was turning the envelope over and over, wondering if it was blessing or curse. Or just an innocuous note. Or even a check. Before I decided to open it, she said, "Things are bad, aren't they?"

"Yeah, they are, Maureen." I replied, slipping the envelope into my inside coat pocket. I thought about Suzie and the judge and quickly pushed them out of my mind. I trusted Maureen, but Pat's five jiggers of Irish whisky weren't enough to carry me through telling the story two more times this morning.

She looked thoughtfully at me, then said softly, "I'm sorry, Casey." She returned to her desk, recognizing this was not a day for playful banter.

I was lost in thought, replaying the case, hunting for a way to get even with Joey when Maureen told me David was available. I knew the way and his door was open. I shut it as he rose from his chair, and we shook hands across the desk. He sat down wordlessly with raised eyebrows.

"You haven't read the paper or you'd know why I'm here, David. Our judge was killed last night by a hit and run driver."

His jaw dropped. I continued before he could talk.

"I'm sure it was no accident. It was the same kind of car as when somebody took a pot shot at me. And that's not all." I steadied myself and thanked God for Pat and the Irish whisky. "They killed a girl I was hiding at my apartment who had given me information on the case."

His face went white.

"I'm convinced it's all tied together because of the trust and what we might uncover tracing Rose's kid." David stood after a moment, walked to his credenza and poured a glass of water. After a sip, he returned to the desk and picked up the phone. "Maureen, get me Judge McNair's office." He sat silently, eyes slightly squinted, jaws clenched, until she rang back. He picked up, nodded, and then spoke.

"Miss Fregossi, this is David Greenberg. I just heard of Judge McNair's death... yes, a terrible tragedy. I hope and pray they find the person or persons responsible. When I met with him day before yesterday, he promised me a special hearing a week from today on possibly reopening an old adoption case...I knew you would be familiar with it. Clearly, things are in an uproar, but has an interim judge been appointed to handle his docket? Hmm, not yet," he said looking at me. "When do you expect to know? ... first of the week!

"Did he have family? Where should we send condolences?"

Additional sympathy entered his voice as he looked significantly at me, "and Miss Fregossi, whatever will happen to you? Will you retain your position? ... my dear Miss Fregossi, you have my sympathy as well." He hung up and spoke directly to me.

"She'll be there until a permanent replacement is appointed, weeks or months away. Hence, the leak will continue. Of course, the temporary replacement will lack the outrage of Judge McNair who was personally offended at having been duped into perpetrating an injustice. We won't know who it is until next week, though Miss Fregossi says they will try to honor the existing docket setting. That means a hearing one week from today, and she'll be right in the middle of everything that we do or say between now and then."

We sat looking at each other, mulling over our next course of action. I spoke first.

"What could we plant that might smoke out the other side, David, something that wouldn't hurt us, but would lead us to the ones she's trying to help?"

"I'm not used to intrigue, Casey, let me think." After a few moments, he suggested, "What about a subpoena to The Home to produce Corporate Minutes from sixteen years ago as well as the Notary Commission of the person who certified Rose's signature on the papers. If they honor the subpoena, it might help our case; if they don't, it isn't crucial. If you get another anonymous call, it might be revealing. If Miss Fregossi is the leak, which she most certainly must be, she may reveal specifics from the court file which will show up in the call."

"Sounds good, do it." I paused for a moment, and then spoke carefully to him. "David, you know don't you, that you and I are targets too?" I didn't want to say it for fear that the good counselor would turn and run, and who could blame him? But he'd been a help, and it was only fair that he knew the risk.

He looked intently at me, and then spoke. "Mr. Stone, don't be misled by fancy suits, fancy office, and legalese. I took an oath when I became a member of the bar. I took an oath when I joined the Army. I meant both. I fervently believe that if the sworn officers of the court do not pursue and protect our freedoms through the zealous pursuit of justice through law, that everything we won in the war is worthless. And as far as personal safety..." He opened a drawer and extracted a polished, engraved, presentation .32-caliber Beretta. "This was given to me by a former client who knew of my admiration for the oldest arms manufacturer in the world, chartered in 1526. I assure you it is not simply a display piece, beautiful though it may be. I was a champion marksman from sixth grade through college and my Army service. In other words, Mr. Stone, while I prefer battles of law and logic, I am perfectly prepared to defend my person with whatever degree of physical force necessary."

It wasn't boasting, it was a statement of fact. When we shook goodbye, I felt differently about David Greenberg, attorney, solicitor and counselor at law—and fellow soldier in the fight for freedom and justice.

Chapter 18

I took the subway back downtown after calling Manny, who hadn't learned anything. I rode all the way to Battery Park and sat for a while, looking out over the water. Lady Liberty seemed to float between sea and sky, shimmering in the distance. Life throbbed in the city behind me and steamed across the harbor in front of me. Thousands of people who didn't know about the deaths of CPA Simon Rosenthal, respected judge Hubert McNair, and Suzie Oh, delicate, beautiful, beloved girl. All were killed because of greed and my stirring up a pot that boiled over. I alternately quivered with rage and grief. After the fifth cigarette, I stood and silently swore to God, Lady Liberty, and my conscience to get a hell of a lot more than even.

I walked back to my apartment and got there as Luther was finishing up. "Gave you an entire new door and metal casement. Anybody who tries to kick this one in will get a broken foot. Brought in a sofa I had in storage till you get a new one. Keep it as long as you like. It was abandoned by that guy on the sixth floor when he got transferred to Chicago last year."

"Thanks, Luther, I owe you."

"No, you don't, Stone. You've been good to me in the past, and I let you down this time. I owe you."

I told him thanks and that it was a good thing he was hardheaded. He gave me the new key with a rueful laugh as he headed for the elevator.

Alias Baby Girl

I looked at the phone a long time before I made the two calls I'd been putting off. One was to Rose; one was to Uncle Chen. All I could promise Rose was our best efforts on behalf of Angel. All I could promise Fu Chen was that he would receive Suzie's body the instant it was released from the morgue, and that I would be at the funeral. I didn't tell him who did it; just that Captain Butler had taken a personal interest in the matter, and he was a damn good cop.

I couldn't think of anything to do on the case except wait on Chiquita and hope she scored big.

Pat's Irish whiskey was just a memory now, and I had a half a day until Chiquita would be there. I got the bottle of Jack Daniels and poured half a glass. I stared at the black and white label—Tennessee sippin' whiskey—Lem Motlow, proprietor—Lynchburg, Tennessee, population 361.

I wondered what Lynchburg was like. It was in a "dry" county, I heard. Funny. How would they know whether they'd made a bad batch if they couldn't drink it? Maybe they were all teetotalers. There were only 361 of them anyway. The ads always showed the workers in bib overalls. They claimed it was a secret recipe, with magic in the spring water, hard maple charcoal filters, and special hickory barrels.

I wondered how Carl rated it against his family's moonshine. He laughed about his Grandpappy keeping "the recipe" secret till he died. He gave it to his oldest son in his will. Carl loved telling the story. "Well, it warn't exactly in the will, 'cause everybody woulda knowd it then. He gave Pappy a clue in the will where to hunt, and Pap found it hid in the Family Bible in Revelations. Revelations! That was a knee slapper! After Pap read it, he burnt it up in the fireplace. I guess he'll pass it on to my oldest brother Jobe, the same way when his time comes."

My glass was empty. I poured another half glass and sipped slowly, looking at the new sofa, but seeing the old one with its cargo of beauty and death, and felt the cold rage building again.

The phone rang. I ignored it. It rang again twice, paused, and then came back. I jumped up, knocking over my chair.

"Stone here."

"Boss, it's me. I'm getting ready to leave for the cleaning crew and thought I'd check on you. Anything from Captain Butler?"

"No."

"Anything from Manny?"

"No."

"Did you talk to Rose?"

"Yeah, finally. And called Suzie's uncle. And met with Greenberg. He doesn't know who the new judge will be or what he'll do about our motion. We decided to subpoena some Home records and see if that produced another anonymous call to Steve."

"Did you go by the office?"

"Yeah, just long enough to look at the mail. Usual stuff, except for one I've been carrying around ever since. Haven't opened it yet...Got a new door and a sofa from Luther."

"You'll have to let me in tonight. Time to run. Wish me luck, Boss."

"Break a leg, girl. I'll be waiting."

I rummaged through my coat pockets till I found the letter.

Chapter 19

I didn't hesitate this time, but ripped open the flap. Inside was a single page that I unfolded with foreboding. It bore three typewritten lines,

They don't know where Rose's kid is.

They'll let you live till you find her.

Sorry about the girl.

The envelope and the message contained no clue as to the sender except that it was dropped off at the Post Office within a couple of hours of Suzie's murder. All I could figure was somebody who couldn't afford to, was helping us anyway.

The late afternoon faded to dusk, then early evening. I had a couple of hours, maybe three, before Chiquita would be back. I was sick of pacing my living room. I needed air, but I didn't need company. When I got to the street, I walked aimlessly. It was better than being inside with Suzie's memory and endless questions without answers. I picked up a sandwich at a deli and ate it just to have something to do.

Jimmy's newsstand was closed, but I bought a paper at the grocery and headed home. No breeze stirred the trash set out on the street. It seemed the city itself was holding its breath, hoping for Chiquita's success.

I had eaten less than half the sandwich by the time I got home and laid the rest on a plate on my kitchen counter. Jack Daniels didn't appeal. I set the sandwich in the Frigidaire and found a Pabst beside the carton of leftover

Moo Goo Gai Pan. I grabbed the beer and slammed the door trying to shut out the sight of that carton and the memory that less than twenty-four hours before, it sat on the coffee table between Suzie and me as we playfully fought over bites from it. I opened the beer with my church key and paced back and forth hardly sipping.

Time had slowed to a stop. I knew it would, and I still couldn't handle it. I tried to read the newspaper, but gave up when I found myself re-reading stories. Every time I looked at the clock, the hands had barely moved.

I was cursing the clock when there was a "shave and a haircut," set of knocks on the door. Through the peephole, I spotted an excited Chiquita. Fumbling with the new lock, it took a moment before I could get it open.

As soon as it was unlatched, Chiquita burst in, leaping into my arms, knocking me backwards. We stumbled onto the new sofa.

"Boss," she said gleefully. "Boss, I think we got some good stuff!"

"Great, Babe," I said as I untangled myself, rising to shut and lock the door. "Let's have it."

She reached into the skirt pocket of her maid's uniform and pulled out a tightly folded packet of carbon copies.

"Look," she said triumphantly.

I took them and spread them out on the table. The first papers were from a case file with periodic entries.

Rose K _____

- Eighteen years old, 6 ½ months pregnant, forced to leave home when refused abortion, no family support.
- Hard worker, easy to direct.
- MD says pregnancy progressing well.
- Crying episodes—expect trouble getting Baby Surrender
- signed.

Mr. M. came by—likes mother's looks, put hold on baby.

$1,000.00 deposit.

- 7½ months. Mr. M here—reviewed MD reports —OK.
- Baby girl born—mother tearful and distraught—signed Surrender only under great pressure.
- M pays $4,000.00 balance of fee and has nurse pick up infant for transport to L.I.
- March 18 —case closed.

"It's obviously our girl, Chick, but it doesn't pin it directly to Menaphy."

"Boss, read the next pages." I didn't have to read far.

April 2
The Home
Regular Quarterly Board Meeting
Chairman Menaphy called the meeting to order. All board members were present. Minutes of the last meeting were read and approved. Administrator's report: both babies born in the last quarter were adopted out. The one born March 1 went to a couple in Brooklyn. The other went to our own Mr. Menaphy just two weeks ago. The most gratifying thing about this job is the continuing interest and support from our Chairman, who commits his money as well as his time and efforts supporting our facility. For the last 10 years, we've always been able to count on him to help us through our tough times. I'm happy to present this Certificate of Appreciation to him. (applause)

"Chiquita—you've done it! The two of these together establish him taking Rose's baby as well as others. Tell me how you got the goods."

She glowed in her maid's uniform as she told the story. "I reported to the cleaning service a half an hour early. I was already in Tia's uniform because we are the same size.

I told the Chief Maid I knew exactly what to do because my aunt had told me it had better look good, and she had better be proud of me when she got back. I listed my duties: empty the trash, dust on top of everything, damp mop floors on my way out, straighten up the reception room, but leave everything just the way I found it in the offices. Do everything Tia does: reception room, secretary's office, head nurse's office.

"The lady was shocked I knew all that and said, 'I was going to put you with one of the regular maids, but I guess I don't have to.'" I said, "But just the same Ma'am, I want you to check my first room and see if it looks good. I want Tia to be proud of me." Chiquita grinned at me. "She bought it, Boss."

"So how'd it go when you got there?"

"They took us to The Home in a van and unlocked the front door. The five of us went in and got our materials from the utility room. I worked as hard as I could on the reception room and when the Chief Maid came back to check it, she said it looked great. Then, she unlocked both offices and said she'd be back in an hour because she had to help another new girl.

"I knew she was just going out back to smoke, because that's what my aunt says she always does.

"As soon as I got in the secretary's office, I checked the file cabinets. All of them were unlocked but one. They contained just bills, receipts and employee time records. When I got to the locked one, I picked it in no time. It was full of these quarterly minutes, but I didn't know which one to check or whether it would matter, so I shut up the office and went to the head nurse's office.

In her office, everything was locked, including her desk. I picked the lock on her desk first and found the cabinet keys right away. They were numbered to match the cabinets. The cabinets were filled with case files, all alphabetical, so it was easy to find the cabinet with Rose's file and unlock it. Her folder was right there—Rose K____. They type everything in duplicate carbon packs, so I took all of the "Patient" carbon copies, gave a quick cleanup of the room

90

and locked the door behind me. I ran back to the secretary's office and pulled the copy of the corporate minutes that you've got in front of you. I got everything in order just in time.

"The Chief Maid was thrilled with my work and tried to hire me as a regular. Better give me a raise, Boss, she said she'd make me Assistant Chief Maid!"

"Hmmm, this may rate a raise. This is great work...even better than I hoped for. Steve will do somersaults over this if we can get it to him so he can legitimately use it. I'd give it to Greenberg if the judge hadn't gotten killed. Only this morning we agreed to ask for a subpoena for just these minutes. Judge McNair would've granted it for sure. Now, we don't even know who his replacement will be, let alone whether he'll be straight or on the take. We've got to worry about that too, since Miss Fregossi may have some influence on who gets appointed directly, or indirectly through mob connections. Jeeze, what a mess! But you've put us two or three runs ahead of the bad guys, girl. Hurray for you.

"Now our problem is to figure out what to do with these papers."

Chapter 20

I called for a cab, walked her down to the first floor and when it arrived, walked her out and watched the cab for a couple of blocks until it turned north. I made some coffee and studied the papers. The caffeine didn't keep me awake. I woke up stiff and groggy, thin morning light shafting through the blinds.

I dumped the old grounds, started a new pot and headed for the shower. Coffee and shower were finished at the same time. I missed Suzie. I tried not to think of her, and then felt guilty for thinking that way. Then I got irritated for feeling guilty. I poured the first cup of coffee and held it out at eye level. "Suzie, I swear I'll get the creeps who got you." The coffee went down bittersweet from my favorite cup, still sparkling clean.

I finished dressing and headed for the office even though it was Saturday. I should've known Chick would be there. I heard her humming before I opened the door.

"May I help you, sir? This is the office of Casey Stone, Private Investigator, and his intrepid Girl Friday, Chiquita Rodriquez. You have problems, we have solutions."

I laughed in spite of myself. "Indeed we do, Girl Friday, but what are you doing here on a Saturday?"

She ran around the desk toward me and threw her arms around my neck. "Because I missed most of yesterday, I'm excited, and that little girl needs our help. I really did good, didn't I, Boss?"

"You did great, Miss Rodriquez. I'm going to take you to lunch. I guess I'll never have a secret the rest of my life, as good as you are picking locks. But then I didn't have any worth keeping anyway."

She gave me an exuberant kiss on the cheek and flitted back to her desk humming away, and continued a letter she had in the typewriter.

I shook my head in amusement, went into my office to check my cheek in the mirror for her Hibiscus Red No. 6. It took a while to wipe it off.

I took the carbon copies out of my coat pocket and laid them on the desk. Why should I be the only one worrying about how to use them? I dialed the precinct and asked for Captain Butler. The desk sergeant connected me immediately.

"Captain Butler here."

"Steve, Casey. Got a minute?"

"Not much more than that. What's up?"

"Greenberg and I met yesterday. He's not running scared. He's with us all the way. That said, I want you to know that I've had a look at copies of Rose's case file from The Home and some of their corporate minutes."

"How'd you get 'em?"

"They were given to me...I didn't go near the place...and they're authentic. I'd bet my license on it."

"You may be doing exactly that by talking to me."

"By lucky coincidence, Greenberg was going to subpoena the very things I've just seen. Taken together, they mean Menaphy got Rose's baby girl and no telling how many others in the past ten years. Can you use that information? If so, do you have to have the documents themselves? If you can't, is your memory as bad as it used to be, so when this information surfaces again, it'll be brand new and have nothing to do with me?"

There was a long pause before the good Captain spoke. "You've seen Rose's file? And it refers to Menaphy?"

"No, it refers to a 'Mr. M,' who checked on her progress several times during her stay there and paid five thousand bucks for her baby girl."

"What else have you got?"

"I've got corporate minutes of two weeks later thanking him by name for taking the baby born the day of Rose's girl, as well as others over the years."

Another long pause. "Time for me to sit down with the D.A. When is Greenberg's hearing on opening Rose's adoption file?"

"This coming Friday unless the new judge changes it."

"It's a good thing this was my duty weekend. We don't have much time. Are you at your office?"

"Yeah, but if I'm out, Chiquita came in today for a while and we're going to lunch together."

"OK, I'll check back."

By noon, we still hadn't heard from Steve. "What do you think, Chick, time for lunch?"

"You bet, Boss! Where are we going?"

"Wherever you want to go, Girl Friday."

"Is it OK to go to Antonio's?"

"Wherever you want. Sounds good to me."

The waiters couldn't keep their eyes off her, and we had superb service and superb food. For two and a half hours we escaped cares and tribulations and were totally absorbed in the seemingly endless procession of culinary delights. After a tiny dessert and coffee, we finally were on the sidewalk on a perfect afternoon. We walked silently for a while.

"Thank you for lunch, Boss."

"It truly was my pleasure, Miss Rodriquez. Good company, good food...you deserved it. Why don't you go on home and enjoy it. Things will hold at the office."

She nodded agreement, and I got her a cab. As I closed the door, I blew her a kiss, which she returned. I watched her cab until it merged with all the other yellow cabs headed north.

I took a deep breath and settled back to a blue mood missing Suzie despite the bright sunlight. I decided to walk off the huge meal and, hopefully, the mood. Forty-five minutes later I was unlocking my office door when the phone rang. It was Steve.

"Been calling for a couple of hours. I talked to an Assistant D.A. that has worked on a lot of cases with questions of probable cause and claims of illegal evidence. He thinks with Rose's affidavit and testimony next Friday, you're going to get that adoption file opened. That will give you the Surrender, a background report on the adopting person or persons, as well as their identity, and confirm the involvement of The Home. He thinks that will give us probable cause for search warrants at both places, The Home and Menaphy's estate. With this much advance notice, we'll have the paperwork prepared before the hearing and simply need a call from you that the file has been opened. We'll have cops at both places before they can begin any cover-up. If we're ever questioned on how we were able to move so fast, we 'll simply note that we 'd had an eye on The Home for years, and you 'll never be mentioned. "

I let out a big sigh of relief and said, "Thanks, Steve!"

"No thanks needed, Casey. This is my job, you know."

Chapter 21

I did something Sunday morning I hadn't done in years: I caught early Mass and listened to the homily. It was about loving your fellow man. I thought of Rose's kid, Simon Rosenthall, and Suzie. I had trouble digesting this lesson. I needed a dose of an eye for an eye. I left the cathedral comfortable in my resolve to right the wrongs and save the State of New York thousands of dollars in trial and incarceration costs. Lost in my grim ruminations, I failed to pay attention to what was happening around me. At noon, in the heart of Manhattan, less than a block from the subway entrance, I turned a corner and a lightning bolt struck the back of my head. As I fell, I sensed my hat flying off, landing beside a white linen pant leg. Then blackness.

Blackness turned to gray. I must have groaned and stirred, because I felt a kick to the gut and heard a scream which must have been mine. Retching, I found my hands tied behind my back. Every heave caused my head to feel like it was bursting.

Two sets of hands picked me up and set me in a chair, and I found my feet were tied as well. We were in a windowless room lit by a single naked bulb overhead. Its weak light didn't reach to the corners of the room. Miami Slim and Sam Napolitano stood side by side.

"Ah, the Bobbsey Twins visit New York City." I barely got it out before Sam smashed my jaw with one of those huge fists, knocking me to the floor. It was concrete and hurt when I landed. They picked me up and put me back on the chair. In a flat, emotionless voice, Slim asked, "Where's the girl?"

"Don't know." Sam hit me on the other side. The concrete pillow evened out the pain to include my whole body. Maybe five, "Don't knows," later, I slipped back into blackness when my head hit the floor.

When I came to, it was in an alley under some cartons. Everything hurt. I sat up shoving boxes aside. Dizziness and nausea washed over me like a wave at Coney Island. I struggled to my feet and leaned against the dumpster. Things settled into a blurry mix of pain and remembrance. I gingerly felt the back of my head and found the lump was covered with dried blood. I guess I'd been here a while. I felt my pockets. Everything was still there, including my wallet. I had money for a cab, if I could get one to stop. I brushed off, straightened my tie and tucked in my shirt. Patted down my hair—hat was long gone, I remembered. I wiped the blood off my mouth as best I could with my handkerchief and headed for the street, regaining my balance as I went. I was at 79th Street and 3rd Avenue. My face was a mess, judging from the reactions of passersby. I made my way over to the IRT Lexington Subway 77th Street Station and caught the southbound.

I resolved not to go to Mass again anytime soon.

Luther's door was open as I tottered by. He bounded out and caught my elbow and helped me to the elevator. He rode up with me, with a quizzical look, but didn't speak. At my door, he produced his master key and ushered me across the threshold. "You gonna be OK, Mr. Stone?"

"I am now. Thanks Luther. Just lock me in."

I painfully shed clothes, letting them lay where they fell, and stepped into the shower. The shock of the cold water blended into the sting of the hot as it hit bruised, scraped and cut flesh from the top of my head to my ankles which had been so tightly bound they were gouged deep. I gingerly felt my face: some loose teeth, a busted lip, sore nose, but not broken. The laugh was on Sam, who was still wearing tape on his schnoz, but I couldn't laugh due to aching ribs and gut.

I don't know how long I stood there, but caught my knees buckling as I drifted off. I turned the spigots off and stumbled to bed without touching a towel.

I may have had a worse Monday morning, but I couldn't remember it. Right side, left side, outside and inside—everything hurt. I gave up trying to move so it didn't hurt and grit my teeth—which made me yelp, as at least five teeth were loose. Even my morning coffee was a chore to get past swollen and cut lips.

A look in the mirror as I gingerly shaved confirmed my suspicions. I looked like a circus clown with bright red lips and mumps. The only good thing about getting roughed up was confirmation that Joey still didn't know where his niece was. I was his only lead and that was the only reason I was alive. It cost me my hat and a lot of pain to find that out. Fortunately, I hadn't taken my Colt to church, so I didn't have to report the loss of my sidearm to Steve.

I decided I would keep this to myself for now, not only because I was so stupid to get caught that way, but it gave me one more reason to clean up Joey and his thugs, and I didn't want to hear a lecture from Steve about abiding by the law. It would take a few days before I'd feel up to doing much, hopefully by Friday when Rose's hearing was scheduled, that is, if the new judge kept the docket as scheduled.

I dug my old hat out of the closet and put it on, carefully avoiding the lump where they rapped my noggin. The walk toward the office loosened me up a bit. I picked up a paper from Jimmy who silently studied my face. As he handed me my change, he asked, "Rough Saturday night?"

I tried to smile and mumbled through fat lips, "This is what can happen if you go to early Mass, my friend. Beware."

He laughed, checked to see if we were alone and leaned across his counter. "Anything I need to look for, Mr. Stone?"

"Two goons from uptown, easy to spot, but I doubt they'll stroll by." I described them and the car they'd used when I got shot at, and asked him to keep his ears open for anything about people hunting for a missing sixteen-year-old girl. He nodded OK, and I waved my thanks as I continued down the block.

I let myself into the office, hung my hat and coat up and started another pot of coffee. I had made it through the first section of the paper and the first cup of coffee when Chick arrived, still aglow from her Friday night success.

She stopped in mid-hello when she saw my face. "Boss, what happened? You look terrible. Are you OK? Was it Joey? Are you hurt bad? Did you tell Steve?"

She finally took a breath and gave me a chance to answer. "Chiquita, this stays just between you and me—not Rose, not Steve...just us." I gave her the rundown and finished with, "Chick, I want you to be real careful. Have you got your .32?"

"In my purse."

"When did you last go to the firing range?"

"Wednesday. I only shot a couple of clips, but it was working smoothly, and I was on target. I cleaned it the next day."

"Good. Joey is getting worried. The hearing is just five days away on Friday. His guys didn't get anything out of me, but wouldn't hesitate to lean on you if they thought I was holding out on them. If the hearing comes off as scheduled, Joey will know, Menaphy will probably already have plans in place to get rid of the girl or move her somehow, and you and I will be dispensable. Till this is over, don't make a move without your pistol and telling me or your family where you'll be."

"OK, Boss. Can I do anything for you right now?"

Before I could answer, the phone rang. "Yeah, you can catch the phone."

"Smarty!" She walked back out to her desk with her customary bounce. "Casey Stone's office. Yes sir, I'll put him right on." Covering the mouthpiece with her hand, she called out, "It's Manny."

I picked up and answered, "It's me, what's up?"

"Casey, are you OK?"

"Well, I got pretty beat up yesterday: no broken bones, lots of loose teeth, lumps on the head, sore ribs...the usual stuff. Why do you ask?"

"There's talk about a three thousand dollar contract on you, double if it happens by Friday."

"You're kidding! I've been told almost the opposite, Manny, that I won't be touched until after Friday. Where did it come from?"

"It didn't come from Joey. It came from a lot higher up. The guy that told me runs some numbers and lives in the neighborhood. He deals with Joey, but hasn't told him. He knows how I feel about that jerk and came to me first. I told him he got free breakfasts here for two weeks."

"Cheap at twice the price, Manny. I'll make it up to you. Is there a hit man?"

"This fellow says they're sending in an outsider, an unknown face, from Chicago. He's due tonight. My guy had a small piece of paper with your photo, your address—everything. He said they were spreading these flyers all around town, and the first guy to finger you gets a five hundred dollar bounty."

"Thanks for the tip, Manny." I hung up and turned to my door. "Listen to this, Chick. There's a price on my head." While I gave her the details, she stood in the doorway worriedly shaking her head.

When I finished, she echoed my caution of a moment before.

"Till this is over, don't you make a move without your pistol and telling me, or Steve, or somebody where you'll be. We're both on the hot seat, Boss."

"You're right. I wish we could watch each other's backs until this is over, but we've got to protect Rose till the hearing. We're going to have to stick to her like flypaper, and I'm not up to swatting a fly right now. I'm going to send you down to her office this afternoon to escort her home and spend the night there. After you get her to work, you can come on in to the office.

We both fell silent. She spoke first. "Not my first choice for a date. I ought to make you do it now, Boss, before you recover enough to be a problem. But you're so beat up, you need the protection more than her. O.K., I'll do it, and maybe tomorrow too."

"Time to check in with Greenberg. Maybe he's heard something."

She went to her desk and dialed. I didn't pay attention to the conversation, but she yelled back to me, "He'll call when he's heard."

I suddenly felt all my aches and pains, and rose stiffly from the desk. "Chick, I'm going to lie down for a while. If I doze off, wake me up if anything happens." I gently sat on the sofa, swung my heels up to one arm, leaned back, loosened my tie and was asleep by the time I settled into the cushions.

Chapter 22

I was swimming up from deep water. Everything was blurry and my arms and legs wouldn't move. The surface was far away. Suddenly I burst into the air and was surrounded by alarm bells. As my eyes and mind focused, I realized it was the office telephone. My head, ribs, arms and legs ached as I tried to sit up on the office sofa. I heard Chiquita saying, "Let me check if he's available, Mr. Greenberg."

I had made it up on one elbow when she stuck her head through the door.

"You awake?"

"Yeah, thanks."

She helped me sit up and struggle to my feet. I reached across the desk to pick up the receiver. "Stone here," I mumbled through swollen lips.

"Mr. Stone, this is Greenberg. I just got a call from the Court Clerk's office confirming the hearing Friday and advising they were mailing confirmations today. They said everyone connected with the case would get notices including The Home, the surrendering mother, the adopting party…who they would not identify, and me as Trustee for the child."

"Did they tell you who the new judge was?" It hurt to talk.

"I beg your pardon?"

I repeated the question as distinctly as I could.

"Are you O.K., Casey?"

"I'll tell you about it in a second. Tell me about the judge."

"Jonathan Law, a retired criminal judge. I've checked on him and don't know if it's good or bad, but when he was on the bench, he was known to be short on tolerance and long on sentencing. I can't imagine that he knows anything about family law, but he was available and was appointed."

"What can I do to help?"

"Not much, Casey, besides making sure Rose is safe and testifies. I'll have to play it by ear, as I am an *amicus curiae*—friend of the court—just trying to honor the terms of the trust and insure that the court is fully informed of all the factors involved. Now what about you?"

"Joey's goons nabbed me coming from Mass yesterday and beat the crap out of me trying to find out where Rose's girl is. So at least they don't know that yet."

"How badly are you injured, Stone?" The concern was sincere.

"Bad enough, but it's nothing I haven't survived before. I'll be O.K. by Friday. Now, the other thing is, I have some confidential information that indicates our motion for the subpoena was right on the money."

"Casey, hold up! Don't say another thing that might put me under an obligation to disclose improperly obtained information to the court."

"I wasn't going to, David. I was going to compliment you on your good instincts with that subpoena and suggest that all parties be put under a restraining order to preserve any and all records and documents. If I understand the proceedings, Menaphy will be there and all parties present will be sworn. Right, Counselor?"

"That's correct."

"If Menaphy was the custodian or adopting party, you'll have a chance to question him under oath, right?"

"Correct again."

"You'll ask all kinds of things, like where she is, the name she uses, who's providing day to day care, where she goes to school, her pediatrician's name, if he has a photo, and stuff like that. Right?"

"Again correct, Mr. Stone."

"When Menaphy gets notice and realizes the file is likely to be opened, he may not wait to find out, but take immediate steps to hide the girl or even worse."

"Hummmm." I could hear him thinking.

"If the file is opened, I've got us covered. The police will be on both The Home and Menaphy's estate with search warrants within minutes. The problem is the time between now and Friday, when Menaphy or Joey put two and two together and move to subtract one. Remember the leak...everybody gets advance warning even before the notices."

"Are you keeping an eye on Miss Kelly?"

"You bet. Chiquita or I will stick with her from now to the hearing except while she's at work, and we won't even let her go outside for lunch until this is over."

"Stone, you said the police are poised to move on The Home and Menaphy, but you didn't say anything about Joey."

"Counselor, I happen to know that Joey is in a bit of trouble with his bosses, and I don't expect much out of him the next few days. On Friday, when he learns what happened to the girl, he still won't know that Menaphy is even more motivated that he is to make sure she doesn't surface. But it won't take a minute before his thug, Sam Napolitano, says to him, 'Menaphy? My brother works security for that guy.' Then we'll be facing a two headed monster."

"Casey, let's stay in close contact till this is over. Let me give you my private number and my home number." We exchanged numbers and hung up.

My hand was still on the phone when it rang again. I picked it up before Chiquita could get it. "Casey Stone, can I help you?" There was traffic noise in the background. The man had an Italian accent, spoke low and deliberately.

"Joey's people are going to off Rose tomorrow morning as she leaves the deli headed for work. People up the ladder from Joey put out a contract on you. The hit man is coming to Newark tonight on the Chicago plane. They plan for him to nail you at Jimmy's newsstand in the morning. After that, the guy will be in your office and work over your girl till she talks, and she will! This guy is so bad they won't even use his name. They call him, 'The Death Angel'."

The connection was broken before I could speak. I gently returned the receiver to the phone and sat for a long time, listening to Chiquita humming to herself in the front office.

I called Fu Chen and told him it was Joey's people who shot Suzie. He was eager to do anything he could to avenge Suzie's death. He told me Joey was in his office and gave me Joey's phone number. I used the same handkerchief over the mouthpiece that I used when I emptied his safe. Sam answered my call with, "Catalano Imports."

"Put Joey on."

"He ain't available. Who's this?"

"Look, Sam, put that worthless piece of crap on the phone. Can't you tell who's calling?"

"Errrrrr, yes sir, hold on."

It was all I could do to keep from laughing out loud. Like I said, Sam was muscle, not brain.

"Who is this?" came Joey's snarl.

"A friend. Shut up and listen, you two-bit punk. The organization is going to terminate you for skimming the weekly take." I paused to see if I had his attention. There was dead silence on the line.

"Felix will take out Sam and then you at supper tonight. If you want to save your worthless hide, you get Sam to take care of Felix in your office before you leave today, then lose your appetite, and you and Sam hit the road to some little Jersey place like Barnegat for a couple of weeks till things cool off. You owe me, Punk. One day, if you take this tip, you'll be around to pay me back the favor." I listened long enough to hear his shallow breathing and hung up smiling grimly.

Sometime later, Mr. Chen called and gleefully told me that Sam took some sheets from the laundry right after my call. A couple of hours later when they thought no one saw,

Sam and Joey carried a long bundle wrapped in the sheets to the dumpster. They left in Joey's car, each carrying a satchel. Chen checked the contents of the dumpster and confirmed that it was the late Felix the Cat. The only thing that could've made him happier was if it had been Sam.

"Thanks, Mr. Chen. We're on the way to making it right for Suzie." If Joey were out of town, he'd miss getting the court notice. If he did go to Barnegat, my cousin would spot them easily. Jack was one-fifth of their police force, and I called to give him a heads up on a large pasty-faced man with a taped up nose and a small ferret-faced guy in a black Ford with Connecticut plates.

I was narrowing the odds.

Chapter 23

We didn't have to worry so much about Rose now that Joey was on the run and Felix was kaput. Still, I felt she needed protection and having Chiquita with her would take care of the problem.

I was exhausted. "Chick, I'm going to lie down again. Don't leave without waking me if I doze off."

She stuck her head around the doorway, nodded, and watched with a worried look as I painfully moved to the sofa.

My ribs protested as I lay down and then I hit the sore spot on my head. She didn't scold me for the curse words. I didn't nap this time. I was in no shape to take on a top-notch hit man who knew everything about me. He had my photo, my addresses, and routines. I didn't know anything about him except the Mob called him "The Death Angel." If I had time, I could probably get a little info from my snitches, but I didn't have the option of choosing time and place. Assuming the accuracy of my informant, tomorrow morning would bring my assassin, ready or not.

I flexed my shooting hand. Fingers were OK, but my wrist was still sore from being trussed up by Sam and Felix. I rolled up to a seated position with a groan and got my Colt, dropped the magazine out, cleared the chamber, cocked and pulled the trigger several times until I was satisfied I could do it normally.

I called Rose at work and told her that Greenberg had asked us to provide round-the-clock protection for her until the trial. She was delighted until I told her it would be Chiquita performing that duty.

"Not you, Casey?"

"Sorry, Rose. Chiquita's on duty for this one."

"But Chiquita doesn't like me. She looks daggers at me. It'll be awful."

"Rose, it's not up for debate. Listen carefully." I told her enough about getting waylaid and the developments about Friday's hearing to pacify her.

"But after the hearing, Casey, will you baby-sit?"

"Sooner or later, Rose. Sooner, I hope. Remember, we may have to jump on the fire engine to rescue Angel. Chiquita will be by your office about 3:00 PM. with her overnight bag."

"I'll welcome her with open arms," Rose said with an exaggerated sigh. I hung up with a chuckle and leaned back in my chair trying to find a position that didn't hurt.

The phone rang. Chick answered then called to me, "It's Captain Butler."

"Yes, Steve."

"Casey, you sound a little funny. What's up?"

"I ran into a door and busted my lip."

"A door, huh?"

"Yeah, I'll be OK."

"Sure there isn't something I should know? Remember, we're on the same side."

"Thanks, Steve. I'll tell you about it later."

"Well, you asked me to check with the precinct working the judge's hit and run. They don't have much, but there were enough witness statements to confirm Connecticut license plates, but nobody got the number...nothing on the driver except he wore a hat and the passenger was in white. I told them it matched up with your drive-by shooters and probably the CPA murder as well. I asked them to keep in touch and promised we would do the same.

"But here's the real news. You're going to love this, Casey! Upper East Side Precinct reports a body discovered in a dumpster by the sanitation boys: tall, thin, white linen suit...apparently died of a broken neck."

"It's got to be Felix, Steve. The only thing bad about it is that I didn't get to do it myself. Has anybody made a positive ID?"

"He was staying in a flophouse near where they found him, and the desk clerk is due at the morgue for the ID as soon as he gets off duty."

"Assuming it's him, Captain Butler, that leaves Joey with just Sam. Anybody seen them?"

"Nobody from the beat cop to the homicide detective has turned up anything. The coroner hasn't made a report yet, but the detective in charge is an old-timer, and he says the body was hardly cold. He figures Joey and Sam were either hit too, or were the ones who did it, because those three were never apart."

"Tell you the truth, Steve, I feel a lot better than before you called. Let me brief you from my end. I've got Chiquita babysitting Rose around the clock. I'm hanging around the office. Greenberg's found out who the new judge is for Friday and tells me he's a retired criminal judge who wielded a heavy hammer in his day. I'll check with my contacts up in Joey's stomping grounds and let you know if I hear anything. The only wild card right now seems to be Menaphy. It may be time to check in with him again."

"Hmmm, Casey, I'd be real careful this go 'round."

I hesitated. I took care of my own problems. This time, however, there were some innocent folks dependent on me, and I wasn't moving at full speed.

"Steve, the Mob has a contract on me and a guy called The Death Angel is due in tonight on the plane from Chicago. I wouldn't mention it, but..."

"I know, Casey, I know. Still I wish you'd told us earlier. We have a good relationship with Chicago. I'll see what I can learn and be in touch."

Chapter 24

I decided to spend the night in the office on the sofa rather than risk travel to my apartment. I had no idea what the hit man looked like, and he knew everything about me. I slept with Betsy cocked with a round in the chamber.

Next morning I snuck out the back way and didn't go anywhere near my usual routes, but headed uptown on the subway and caught a coffee and a bagel on the way to pick up my car.

I called Menaphy's secretary and told him it was an emergency. I needed a few minutes of Mr. Menaphy's time and it had to be this morning. He put me on hold and came back with a reluctant, "Eleven o'clock, Mr. Stone, for no more than fifteen minutes."

Ten o'clock found me motoring through the ritzy section of Long Island. I had deliberately insisted on a different time of day, just to check any differences in the routines at the estate.

The gate had two different guards who really gave my beat up face the once over before waving me in. Everything seemed the same: manicured sweeping lawns, fine buildings, raked white gravel drive. There was no visible activity at the pool, tennis court, or the playground.

I was escorted down the hall to the patio once again where, to my surprise, I found an animated game of field hockey between two teams of girls, the oldest in her mid-teens. I watched intently as they ran about in their contrasting uniforms with numbers on their jerseys and matching shorts. I had never seen field hockey. It was strictly a tony girl's school game, far from my experience. But hockey is hockey, and the girls played with effort, enthusiasm, and skill, their sticks flashing down to give the hard rubber ball some smart licks.

The valet remembered that I took my coffee black and disappeared into the home when I declined any food. The longer I watched, the more my eye was drawn to the captain of the white team. Her long blonde hair was tied up in a ponytail and her shin guards didn't hide the beauty of her legs. She was constantly on the move with grace and quickness, and kept up a steady stream of chatter to her teammates, giving commands, corrections and compliments. The longer I watched, the more I saw a teenage Rose. Her teammates called her Angela.

My concentration was interrupted by a brisk, "Good morning, Mr. Stone. What is the urgency that brings you here today?"

As I turned to greet him, he was visibly shocked at my appearance and took a half step back.

"Sorry, Mr. Menaphy, a hazard of the profession. I wish I could say, 'you ought to see the other guy,' but this time I definitely took it on the chin, as you can see."

"My word!" was all he could say, over and over.

I broke into his shock. "Delightful game on the lawn, sir. I don't know much about field hockey, but these girls play as hard as the pros."

"Why, yes, Mr. Stone. You may have noticed the building to the west. I have nurtured homeless girls for decades. What you are looking at is one of their favorite pastimes, though I must admit I find it a bit brutal on occasion. No wonder their tutors insist on protective gear."

As he looked toward the field, I eyed him carefully. His face gradually lost the reaction to my bruised and swollen face and turned to warmth and even lust as he became lost in watching lithe young bodies dashing about. One of the girls chased an errant ball up to the patio and noticed him. "Hi, Uncle Joe." He woke from his thoughts and waved to her, then recalling me, resumed the role of master of the house and said, "Your mission, Mr. Stone. What is the emergency?"

"As you can see, Mr. Menaphy, I've been on the receiving end of some rough treatment. My employer warned me about resistance to his move to the U.S. market, and I, frankly, thought he was overstating the case. No longer. I have reported to him, and he thought it was only fair to inform you of the situation as you had agreed to meet with him and now we find it is not as confidential as we thought. In other words, my employer is an honorable man and wanted to let you know and give you the opportunity to decline any association with him."

His face instantly went hard in a way I never thought that patrician visage could. It must have been the same as the Roman emperors when they condemned enemies of the state to crucifixion. His eyes, once limpid blue, were flinty and his voice grated. "Mr. Stone, tell your Mr. Cooper that it will be a frigid day in Hades before some second rate maneuver like this causes me to turn tail and run. I am the master of my own fate. My decisions are honored nationwide. have a security force the equal of some armies. These people don't know who they're dealing with."

I had him. "Perhaps it would be wise to educate me, sir, so I can reassure Mr. Cooper that all is under control, personally and professionally, especially as I got caught off guard."

For the next fifteen minutes, he explained every aspect of his security force, their routines, the cameras and alarms on the property and especially the security on the main house.

"What about the other buildings, the stable, and the dock," I asked.

"We've never had any trouble at the dock and the lights come on automatically at dark. The stable houses my automobiles and the upper level provides lodging for my valet and his family. He is also my driver. The other building is the dormitory for the girls and no one is supposed to be there except the girls and three housemothers. The security force drives the perimeter in golf carts every hour and half hour. I think you'll agree it is more than adequate."

I enthusiastically agreed and bid him goodbye.

Driving back to Manhattan, it seemed the only areas not well covered by Menaphy's security were the side borders of his property where they entered the Long Island Sound, and with good reason: they were rough, rocky, and remote from anything else on the estate.

I arrived at the garage and Carl met me to take the car. Opening the door, he looked at my mangled face and simply said, "Seen a lot of that when somebody didn't honor a territory back home. Iffin you need a driver or a backup, I ain't forgotten how to help. I got a carry permit, and I'm good with a rifle. I ain't so good with a pistol. I don't go huntin' trouble, but won't let no friend down neither."

"Carl, do you still go fishing out in the Sound?"

"Yep. Got a twenty-foot dory. Don't get out as much as I'd like."

"How would you like to take a nighttime cruise up the Sound?"

"When?"

"How 'bout tonight?"

"I can do that."

"I'll pay for the gas, Carl. But before you commit, I got to tell you there's a bit of risk in it."

"Wouldn't be no fun otherwise."

"Hear me out, my friend, you need to know what you're getting into." I laid out my plan: boat up to the southern boundary of Menaphy's estate, tie off out of sight, wade in or crawl over those rough boulders. Dash across the field to the dormitory, counting on lazy guards and an unlocked door from the playground. Locate the girl. Play it by ear from there.

"All I'm asking you to do, Carl, is pilot the boat and wait for me. If I'm discovered and you hear alarms, you take off without any lights."

He sat silent for a few moments. "Mr. S, I know I don't look like much, but I was the best 'coon hunter in East Tennessee. I see real good in the dark, and I got good instincts. I never got lost in Germany day or night. If I'm in this, I'm in all the way. I'm pretty stout iffin it comes to somebody jumpin' us, but maybe you better 'fess up to what we're doin'?"

I looked at him and was shamed. "Carl, here's the story." I didn't use names, but I told him about Rose and her baby, The Home, the adoption racket, Menaphy's farm of girls, and the fear that this girl would be killed as soon as he learned of Friday's hearing, or Joey put her and Menaphy together. Joey would profit one million dollars by her death; Menaphy would keep his reputation and slavery operation going.

"Hellfire, Mr. S, this ain't nothing but cleanin' up a cesspool. When do we go?"

"It has to be tonight, because court notices have been sent and will arrive no later than Wednesday."

"I keep the boat gassed up, Mr. S. Let's do it."

"Done, Carl. When and where do I show up?"

We agreed on 9:00 PM at a dock he rented on the East River. It would take at least two hours to get there. I handed him a c-note for gas and extra tanks and headed for the office. It was early afternoon and the city was its usual busy self.

I didn't enter my building, but walked by, searching the area for anyone who looked out of place. I ducked in a deli, bought a newspaper and some custard, as it hurt to chew. I took another quick look up and down the street and entered my building. There was no one in the hall and no one in the elevator when it arrived at my signal. I punched in the floor below mine and checked the hall before I got out. A secretary passed on the way to the restroom and said a low "ouch" when she saw my face. I tipped my hat and ducked in behind her till I got to the stairs. They were clear and so was my own hallway. I quickly let myself in and hung a "Closed" sign on the door, locking it behind me. I locked the inner door to my office as well. I washed some aspirin down with water from our cooler and sat down at my desk to write Chiquita a note.

Chapter 25

Chiquita and Rose were going to be joined at the hip for the next three days. I probably wouldn't see Chick and didn't want to talk about things over the phone. I wrote out my plans in detail, put them in her desk and locked the drawer.

I wrote a will. It was simple, straightforward and plain. I gave everything to Chiquita. I folded it and put it in an envelope, sealed it and wrote on the front, "Open only upon my death," and signed beneath it. I put it into my right desk drawer. She wasn't likely to see it. If things went well, I'd retrieve it unopened, and she'd never know. If it didn't go well, I knew she'd handle things as well as anybody could.

The aspirins were helping. I lay down on the sofa. It was eight hours till I met Carl to boat to the Menaphy estate. Would I get to shore OK? Would some staff be awake as well as the security men? Would the door to the playground be open? If it were locked, how long would it take me to pick it? How would I find the girl I was looking for? I was sure they bunked at least two to a room. What if they had an open dorm arrangement? All I knew was her appearance in broad daylight in a hockey uniform and the name, "Angela." Neither one of those things would help in the dark. Worse yet, what would happen if some girl screamed at a midnight intruder, as any reasonable girl would? What was I thinking?

It was about 10:00 PM, and we were motoring swiftly up the Sound. I'd never been on the water at night and despite the tension of our mission, was fascinated by the starry sky above and the fluorescence of the wake behind the boat. Carl seemed at home navigating in the dark, identifying landmarks to me as we worked our way north. I had described the estate to him, particularly its pier with lights, boathouse and yacht. He didn't seem concerned about finding it.

The water was smooth and there were no boats close to us. He reached under the gunwale and brought out three watertight cases. The first held a 12-gauge shotgun, the second a 30.06 rifle, and the third a Smith & Wesson police special .38. "All of 'em are loaded, but there's nothing in the chambers." As he showed each one to me before returning it to its case, he calmly described which one might be used, depending on the situation.

"Carl, I don't want you getting in trouble here. This is my problem, not yours. I just signed you up for a boat ride."

"Right, Mr. S. But I'll tell you what happens to guys diddling little girls back home. We take 'em out in the woods and talk to 'em right plain. If they repent, we only geld 'em. If they don't, well, we also take a gun and a shovel along and that problem is laid to rest. I had a sister once't ..." He was lost in thought for a few moments, then continued, "So, Mr. S. I kindly think this is everybody's problem."

I gripped his shoulder for a moment, and then patted him on the back.

"Understood, my friend, understood," I murmured over the low growl of the motor.

It was easy to spot Menaphy's estate from the water. The immediate grounds around the house were lit from the rooftop and there were some lights on the dock, but the edge of the property was comfortably dark. Carl turned off his running lights and cut the engine back to a low idle. About thirty feet from the rock jetty, he killed the engine and we drifted slowly up to it. He eased over the side, found footing, and tied us to one of the steel rods holding the boulders in place. He dropped some bumpers over the side to protect the boat and stood waist deep steadying it for me. The water lapped quietly against the side of the boat. The only other sound was insects in the trees and shrubs along the boundary fence leading to the jetty. I slipped over the side as gently as I could, feeling every kick and blow from my Sunday work over. My feet touched bottom, but immediately slipped out from under me, and I went under. Carl grabbed my shirt and pulled me toward him, quietly laughing as I surfaced choking and spitting.

"You OK, Mr. S? I'd hate to explain a drowned P.I. like yourself to the Manhattan Police. You got a will?" he asked jokingly.

My irritation at taking an unexpected dunking gave way to amusement at the absurdity of it, and I had to suppress open laughter. The shock of the cold water had erased everything, including my soreness and tension. OK, OK We're Abbott and Costello, and I just took a pie in the face.

I had left my Colt in the boat, but was taking my slapjack.

"I'll work my way up the boundary, then make a dash for the playground when it looks safe and go in that back door. If it's locked, I'll pick it. The sleeping rooms are likely on the top level, and it will take me a while to find the girl. If I'm gone more than half an hour, it's a problem. If things go sour, you take off and contact Captain Butler at the Greenwich Village Precinct. OK?"

"I got it, Mr. S. Be careful."

I checked my pockets: no ID—though Menaphy and his valet would know me by sight—lock picking kit, small flashlight, slapjack, a small roll of duct tape. Nothing shiny on my black outfit.

I clambered along the boulders and paused in the shadows until the golf cart whirred by about thirty yards away. Two unfamiliar guards were smoking and chatting about some broad they had shared last weekend. I heard enough to want to hear the rest of the story.

When they were out of sight, I ran to the playground, slipped through the gate and knelt at the back door of the dormitory. When I tried the handle, it was locked, but it was a standard door with simple locks, and I was inside in moments. I shut it gently behind me with the lock off. There was no alarm system on it that I could see or hear. Kneeling inside, I paused to get my bearings. The only sound was the distant sound of Doris Day singing on the radio. I was in the cafeteria. Emergency lights glowed over all the doorways. There was an open entrance to the hall on the far side of the room that was also aglow with emergency night-lights.

I crept through the tables and benches and checked the hallway before entering. The radio came from around the corner of the hallway to the right. I went the other way and soon found the stairs, started up, paused at the landing, and continued to the main floor. It appeared to be administrative offices and classrooms. The radio had faded to silence, and I became acutely aware of the sound of my breathing, rubber-soled shoes, and the faint rustle of my clothes.

I continued up the stairway to the next floor and found myself facing a wall that had a fire escape plan under a red glowing emergency light. I crept over to it and realized it was a floor plan directing occupants to exit at the two ends and the middle staircase I came up in the event of an emergency.

I stilled my breath and heard the soft undercurrent of sleeping people in both directions. I checked my watch—ten minutes had passed. I crept over to the chart and found twelve rooms, most with two occupants written in and a dorm mother at either end. A common shower and bathroom was near the center. It only took a few seconds to locate "Angela", the only name on the room located next to the bath in the center.

I easily made my way and tried the doorknob. It had no lock, and I slipped in quietly, closing it behind me, only to hear a sharp gasp.

The room was dimly lit from the security lights flooding the front of the building, and I saw the girl sitting upright in her bed in a plain white gown. I chanced it.

"Angela, I'm a friend. I'm sorry I frightened you. Can we talk for a second?"

After a moment, she whispered in a quaking voice, "I thought it was Mary. We sometimes sneak into each other's rooms, even though they whip us if we get caught. Who are you?"

"My name is Casey. I'm a private investigator. A lady hired me to find her baby...well, kid now...she was forced to give up years ago. I think that girl might be you. How old are you?"

"Sixteen."

"What is your birthday?"

"March 15," and added, "I'm the only sixteen-year-old here."

"What do you know about your parents?"

"Nothing, except they told me I was abandoned and The Home took care of me until Mr. Menaphy brought me here as a baby. All the girls here came from The Home. Do you know my mother?"

"Maybe it's Rose, the lady I mentioned. Do you know anything about your father?"

"They said he died before I was born and they didn't know anything about him."

"Angela, you might be in great danger because of things you don't know about. Would you come away with me?"

"I hate this place. It's worse than jail. I..."

She was interrupted when the door swung open behind me, the light flipped on and a harsh female voice crowed, "Ah hah! I caught..." Her voice froze as she spotted me.

I leaped on her cupping my hand over her mouth. She was strong, and the struggle awoke every hurt, bruise and scrape I had, but I knew that my life and the girl's life hung in the balance. As we thrashed about the room, I glimpsed Angela plastered against the wall on the backside of her bed, mouth open, and eyes wide. The woman and I finally stumbled across the bed, and I was able to grab my slapjack and give her a sharp blow on the head. She went limp.

Angela sprung alive at the same moment and leaped across us to the light switch and plunged the room back into darkness. I heard her shut the door quietly.

"As you all right, sir?"

"Yeah, kid," I gasped. "Do you think anybody heard?"

"No, Miss Jones has some whiskey every night before bed, and she couldn't hear us over her snoring."

"Who is this one?"

"Miss Elmore. She's mean."

I groped for my duct tape and quickly bound her wrists behind her back, then her ankles, and finally her mouth. My eyes were adjusting to the dark by the time I finished.

"Well, kid, she got a good look at me and she may have heard enough of our conversation to know what we were talking about. Do you want to stay or go?"

"Go!"

"Quick! Put on clothes and carry your shoes till we get outside."

She flitted back and forth in the shadows between closet and bed while I cracked the door slightly and watched the hall. In a moment, she said, "I'm ready."

"We're going down the middle stairs and out the cafeteria door to the playground. When it's clear, we'll run to the jetty on the left where I have a friend with a boat. Stay right with me, do exactly as I say and if we're spotted, you run like crazy and I'll deal with the guards. Got it?"

She nodded. She had her shoes in one hand and a stuffed bear under the other arm.

Within moments, we were in the playground, and I locked the door behind us. There was nothing to be heard but insects and a distant ship's horn.

I glanced at my watch. The golf cart was due, but wasn't in sight. It was go now or wait until it passed. Every moment brought greater risk of discovery. I grabbed her shoulder and whispered in her ear. "See the jetty?" I felt her nod. "My friend is Carl. He's looking for us. Run and crawl out the rocks as fast as you can. He'll see you and put you in the boat. I'll be right behind. OK?" I felt her nod again. "I saw you run in that hockey game this morning. Give it all you've got. Ready?" I felt her tense. "Go!" I whispered and gave her a push on the back.

She was gone in a flash, exactly as I instructed. As I took a last look around, the lights of the golf cart swept up from a dip in the border of the property. Cursing under my breath, I hugged the ground and watched as it approached, passed the playground, and continued near the jetty, then the dock. As soon as it neared the jetty on the other side, I ran as quickly as I could and reached the rocks. They were jumbled, sharp, and slick where the water reached. I groaned with each slip and twist. I couldn't see any sign of Carl and the boat. Then behind me, I heard a shout and lights swept over the rocks. I saw a glint ahead and heard Carl's voice, "Hurry up Casey. They're comin'!"

The end of his sentence was cut off by the sound of a shot behind me and a shout, "Down here!" The next thing I heard was the boom of Carl's 12-gauge followed by screams and strings of curses well behind me. The flash of the gun led me the final fifteen feet. Carl had already cast off the lines and was pushing away from the rocks with an oar. I jumped into the water and grabbed the oar he stuck out for me. He dragged me into the boat where I rolled on the flooring clutching my ribs and trying to breath. I could feel the engine roar into life and the boat banked sharply into the darkness.

All the injuries of the past two weeks flooded my consciousness, together with the smell of hot motor oil, gasoline, seasoned wood—and lavender soap. I forced my eyes open and realized Angela was cradling my head in her lap, crying softly, and patting my cheek.

The boat planed and we were running full throttle without lights. I could only dimly see Carl's silhouette against the sky sweeping the horizon ahead and glancing behind.

I tried to sit up and grunted with the pain. As soon as I could take a breath, I said, "It's OK, kid. You did better than I did." I noticed she was soaking wet and shivering in the wind still clutching her bear. "There're slickers in that box behind you. Get us two. We've got a long trip ahead of us." Sniffling, she did what I told her, and then snuggled up to me leaning against the prow of the boat.

Minutes passed, Carl leaned down and shouted through the wind, "I don't see anything following us. Gonna keep runnin' wide open, though."

The droning motor, dull pain, and stress of the past few days took their toll. I couldn't sleep, but I wasn't fully awake until Carl cut the engine back.

"Mr. S, we're comin' into dock."

I groaned as I straightened out and gently laid the sleeping Angela down. All was quiet at the dock. I looked at my watch. Two o'clock AM. What was I going to do with a sixteen-year-old girl when I had a Chicago hit man lying in wait for me in front and probably an enraged Menaphy and security force behind me?

"Mr. S, it's pretty late. Why don't you stay in the small hotel next to the garage? We have a deal with them for out of towners who rent a car from us. I know the desk clerk and I'll vouch for you being legit even though you'uns look like river rats. It might be better if you were Mr. Smith and his daughter who got held up. That will help explain your face."

"Thanks, Carl. I don't think I can make it home tonight with her."

Chapter 26

Wednesday morning came too quickly. It took a minute to remember why I was on a couch in a hotel room with a kid sleeping soundly in the bed. I got up and made my way to the bathroom as quietly as possible and steamed myself back into a semblance of humanity. I threw the shower curtain back, gently toweled off and wrapped it around my waist, wiped the mirror off and leaned forward to evaluate the damage. The "mumps" had gone down. My upper lip was recovering. The lower lip, which had split on Sam's first blow was still swollen enough to give me a classic two-year-old's pout. My bruises were yellowing a bit, giving my whole face an unhealthy pallor.

As I was gingerly checking the lumps and bruises on my rib cage, the door opened and Angela stepped in.

"Whoa girl. One at a time in here."

"I've seen men before," she said dully.

"Angela, that may be, but not again, not me, not until you've grown up and want to."

She stopped dead, looked up at me with inquiring eyes until they got the answer that it was the truth. Then they filled with tears and ran over, her head slowly sinking into her hands, shoulders heaving. I held her for a long time.

Finally, her muffled voice came through arms and towels, "Is that really true Mr. Casey?"

"Kid, I'll die before you get used again."

She didn't look up. "It was awful Casey. When Mr. Menaphy first told me what I had to do with him, I was

123

Robert W. Godwin

horrified at the thought and refused.   He told me I had to, or
they'd lock me in the storeroom, and they did.   It's in the
basement of the dorm.   No windows, no lights.   You can't
tell how long you've been there.   They wouldn't give you
real food.   Just some water and some leftover rolls.   Some
of the girls screamed and screamed until they couldn't make
any sound at all when they got put in there.   Everybody in
the dorm could hear them.   Miss Elmore, the one you hit,
would laugh and threaten us with being locked up too.

"I was there a long time before I finally decided to do
anything he wanted.   The next time Miss Elmore came to
check on me, I told her.   Then Mr. Menaphy himself came
and made me tell him to his face.   He said, 'Fine, Angela.   I
want you to settle down for a couple of days, get cleaned up,
and I'll send for you.'   And that's how it started, Casey.   I
was twelve.   After a few times with him, he made me go
with his overnight guests.   It was horrible.   I pretended I
was somewhere else and it was some other girl having to do
those things."

I was chilled by her words and held her tight as I recalled
Carl's mountain justice.   Even that would be too good for
Menaphy.   After a few moments, she looked up and simply
said, "Are you done in here?"

"Yes, sweetie, it's all yours."   I stepped through the
door, pulling it closed behind me.   I dressed in the same
clothes I'd gone swimming in the night before, and
wondered what to do next.   I had to stash the girl, but I also
had to make sure she was the right one.   Rose had always
referred to her lost daughter as "Angel" and this one was
named Angela, a good sign.

As I was cinching my belt, she came out in her own towel
trailing steam.   I couldn't take my eyes off her.   She was a
vision of fresh, innocent beauty no matter what had
happened to her before.

"OK, Mr. Rescuer, turn around."

I blushed and said to the wall as I turned around, "Righto
kid.   Keep that attitude for the next five years.   Can you
listen while you dress?"   I didn't wait for an answer.   "I'm
not absolutely sure who your mother is, but you look a lot

124

like the lady who hired me to find her daughter. She's been grieving for sixteen years…for a girl your age, with the same birthday. Where did your name come from?"

"All they ever told me was that when Mr. Menaphy got me, the papers said 'Angel,' but he didn't like that and changed it to Angela."

"Kid, that's about a lock, because your mother always called you Angel and does to this day when she talks about you."

Still facing the wall I said, "Stay here while I go make some phone calls and get us something to eat. Lock the door behind me and don't unlock it for anybody unless you hear Carl or me. If somebody knocks but won't answer, run and lock yourself in the bathroom and get in the tub. Even if somebody shoots through the door, they can't hit you there.

"Shoots through the door?! Why would anybody try to hurt me?"

I realized she was still in the dark. "If you're who I think you are, your mother had you when she was about seventeen. Your daddy didn't die. He ran off and left her. He got a conscience later though and several years ago started a trust fund and wrote a will giving everything to you if you were alive and could be found. If you were gone, it goes to your dad's brother who has become a junior mobster and would kill you in a minute to get the trust fund that is about a million dollars now.

"It wasn't until the past week or so that we found you'd been born at The Home, and adopted by someone, probably Mr. Menaphy. Then we found out what he'd been doing to you and the other girls, and knew that he couldn't afford for that to come out, so you were in danger there as well. The lawyer for the trust fund has started court proceedings to open the adoption file and Mr. Menaphy will learn about that today. That's why we had to get you out last night."

She listened wide-eyed and silent, her damp blonde hair falling to her shoulders. After a few moments, she said, "So my mother is alive, and hunting for me?"

"Yeah, if it's her, kid. She wants you more than anything in the world. She says there hasn't been a day in the past sixteen years she hasn't prayed for you."

"I've prayed too, but I never believed I had a mother out there. I still can't believe it."

"We've got to make sure you stay safe. You're a target, but so am I for trying to find you."

I patted her on the shoulder, stepped into the hall and waited until I heard her throw the lock, then slipped down to the street and ducked over to the garage. Carl was with a customer, but nodded to me, and strolled over when he was free. "How's the girl?"

"Good. I gave her the story, and she is eager to meet her mother. I hope it really is Rose. The kid's life on the estate was even worse than we thought. He started her at age twelve."

Carl grunted. "Wish it had been him instead of those two guards on the far end of that buckshot. What now?"

"Well, both she and I are targets. We have to lay low till Friday's hearing at least. Have you seen today's paper?"

"No, Mr. S. There's one in the office, but I've been runnin' as fast as I can this morning and likely won't get to see it until bedtime."

"I promised the girl some eats, Carl. Can I pick you up some coffee and a bagel?"

"Bagel would be nice. We've got plenty of coffee in the office."

I didn't see anybody on the street that looked like "The Death Angel." Half a block west brought me to a deli where I loaded up on bagels, spread, and some orange juice for the girl. I got myself a large coffee—I've drunk garage coffee before.

The street still looked OK, and I carried two bags and my coffee back to the hotel and entered the front. The lobby was empty except for a new desk clerk, who took one look at my face and reached under the desk.

"Easy fellow. I'm a friend of Carl's next door at the garage. Daughter and I came in late last night after I got held up. See, here's my room key." I slid it across the desk, and he picked it up cautiously keeping the other hand below the desk, flipped through the registry and reluctantly slid it back.

"Smith, huh, with a daughter?"

"That's right. Check with Carl. He'll vouch for us."

"I think I'll do just that."

"OK if I go on up to the room while you do? A minute ago, he was on a dead run parking the morning rush hour."

"Yeah," he said grudgingly, and watched me all the way up the stairs.

There was no one on my hall and a few brisk steps brought me to our door. I knocked lightly and when I saw a flicker at the peephole said softly, "It's Casey."

The chain and lock slid open, and I stepped in as she quickly closed and locked the door behind me. She pawed through the bag the instant I set it down.

"Mmmm! Bagels and cream cheese. And orange juice...my favorite! How did you know?"

"Hey, I'm a P.I. I know things," I said, reluctant to admit that's all they had. "Eat up, kid. I didn't get to make my calls, so same routine with the door, and I'll be back in fifteen or twenty minutes." I took one deli bag and my coffee and opened the door carefully.

"OK," she mumbled through a big bite of bagel, locking the door behind me.

The desk clerk made a point of ignoring me as I passed through the lobby. After a quick look up and down the street, I slipped over to Carl's. He looked up from the engine bay of a large Buick and nodded OK, as I pointed to the office and held up the deli bag of bagels.

I shut the office door behind me and dialed up Lawyer Greenberg. "Everything still on for day after tomorrow, David?"

"Yes, and listen to this. I got a call from a lawyer for The Home pumping me for information about Friday's hearing. At first he was low key. 'Mr. Greenberg, what's your interest in an old adoption file? This isn't your usual area of practice.'

"I told him I was searching for a girl who was the beneficiary of a testamentary trust and our investigation led us to The Home and to this particular file which might give us her identity and location. He jumped right on it, Casey. *'That's shaky legal ground'*, Mr. Greenberg said. *'There's a strong expectation of privacy on the part of the biological mother, the adopting parties, and The Home itself, not to mention the child.'*

I told him I understood and looked forward to working with him in such an interesting case. I didn't tell him that we had the bio mother and were going to question the legitimacy of the adoption. Then I asked him if he expected to have anyone there from The Home. I could just see him licking his lips, Casey, as he said, *'The Chairman of the Board is J. K. Menaphy, a name I expect you recognize. He'll be there on behalf of the Board, and we have been directed to resist the Motion with every means at our disposal.'*

"David, you do think the judge will open the file, don't you?"

"Yes, Casey, but remember we're dealing with an unknown judge on a case that certainly has two sides. We won't know until the judge rules. You get Rose safely to my office tomorrow afternoon to prepare her testimony, and I'll worry about the hearing."

"When do you want her there?"

"She's due at 2:00 PM."

"We'll have her there on time, David. What happens if Joey doesn't show up for the hearing?"

"If he got notice, the judge will ignore his absence. If he didn't, there might be an argument on his behalf. My position in representing the estate and the trust is that Mr. Catalano is an unnecessary party who has no legal interest in the matter unless the primary trust beneficiary is shown to be dead or cannot be found within the allotted time, neither of which can be determined until she's identified by opening the file."

"Counselor, don't worry about Joey and don't worry about the girl—she's safe. I may be hard to reach between

128

now and getting Rose to your office tomorrow. If you need to get in touch with me, leave a message with Captain Butler at the Village Precinct or Carl at the 58th Street Garage." I gave him both numbers and realized as I hung up that I was long overdue to talk to my favorite cop.

"Captain Butler's off duty till tomorrow," the desk sergeant said. I told him I'd call back.

Manny was a different matter. He said his informant told him over breakfast that the hit man was in town and that Joey and company had disappeared. He couldn't describe the hit man, but told Manny that everybody was afraid of him and everybody was out looking for me.

My next call went to Pat.

"Pat's Bar and Grill."

"It's Casey, Pat. Don't use my name."

"Yes sir, Mr. Smith. Let me check if anybody's turned in a missing hat." I heard him lay down the receiver and walk toward the other end of the bar. He picked up the other receiver and yelled to the bus boy to hang up the first one. He spoke softly, and I could hear him rummaging around under the bar.

"Yesterday and today, there's been a steady stream of new faces. One will come in, sit where he can see the whole place, order one beer and nurse it for an hour. Then he leaves without a word and without a tip. A couple of hours later, same song, next verse. These guys don't fall for barman chitchat. One's here now." Then he said loudly, "Don't find it, sir."

"Pat, if they're working your place, they're watching my office and apartment too. I'm hiding out in Midtown at least until the hearing day after tomorrow. Steve's off today. If you need to reach me, leave a message with Manny or with Rose. Chiquita's babysitting her day and night until the hearing."

"I'll keep an eye out for it Mr. Smith. Take care."

I leaned back in Carl's swivel chair, finished the last bite of my bagel and downed the last sip of coffee. In addition to the telephone, Carl's old metal desk was covered with trays of papers, a mat covered with phone numbers of auto parts stores, wreckers, coffee stains, and an unemptied ash tray. There was a beat up old green file cabinet in one corner and the wall to the left of the desk was covered with hooks numbered one to one hundred, most of which had key rings hanging from them. The coffee maker looked like it had last been washed about VE Day, but the aroma was tempting. There were a few ceramic cups beside it that made the coffee pot look clean. I stuck with my paper cup from the deli and poured myself half a cup just as Carl came in.

He stood wiping the grease off his hands with a red rag and then tossed it into a cardboard box in the corner filled with its brethren.

"Pour me a cup in the brown mug," he said.

"Which brown one, Carl? Don't you have a sink around here?"

He laughed and grabbed the last bagel and sat across from the desk in a metal chair beside a small table buried under old *Hot Rod* and *Motorcycle* magazines. I handed him a cup and asked, "Don't you want to sit in your own chair?"

"Naw, this here's fine. Plus it gives me a better view of the calendar." I turned, following his eyes, and saw the classic auto garage pin-up girl giving us a big smile as she held an air cleaner. She had on some short shorts and nothing else besides the ribbon in her hair. There were at least two things I liked about her.

"They have girls like that back in Tennessee, Carl?"

"Well, Mr. S, maybe we'll make a trip down there someday, and you can see for yourself."

As he finished his bagel and coffee, I brought him up to date on what Manny had told me and the guys staking out Pat's bar looking for me. "Carl, we're in Room 103 at the hotel, and I've told the girl not to let anybody in besides you or me. She'll check you through the peephole before she unlocks. There's a new desk clerk this morning who gave me the once over, but backed off when I told him you'd vouch for us. I'm going to pick up a few magazines for the girl and then run some errands. I'd appreciate it if you could check on her in a couple of hours if I'm not back."

"Sure, Mr. S, I'm here all day, but I usually have a couple of slow spells before and after lunch.   Tell her I'll be up to check."

Chapter 27

I cautiously made my way to a newsstand and surveyed magazines I'd never looked at before: magazines full of stories of thwarted and successful love affairs, endless varieties of facial applications, excited articles about frilly garments, breathless ravings about movie stars. I heaved a sigh and bought four of the most colorful covers and headed back to Angela. She unlocked the door at my knock and squealed with delight at the magazines. I told her Carl would check on her while I was out. "Sure, great," she said as she flipped through the first magazine.

"Be careful, kid. Don't get careless on me."

"Sure, OK, Casey. When did you say you'd be back?"

"Should be a couple of hours. I'm serious kid...be careful!"

I slipped out and was lucky to catch the first cab I flagged. I had him drop me off a couple of blocks from my office and sneaked down the alley and into my building through the service entrance. I took the freight elevator up to the storage room on the floor above mine and worked my way down the back stairs to my floor. The small window in the door with embedded chicken wire reinforcement didn't let me see much, but I could see the clear shadow of a fedora and a guy sitting on the window ledge at the end of the hall.

The door was hinged on the left so I could snap it open and be shielded by its fireproof metal bulk. Whether I wanted to or not, I couldn't get to my office without dealing with this guy. I didn't like the idea of retreat, so I thumbed off the safety, took a deep breath, and hit the push bar on the door.   I slid to a knee with Betsy's 45-caliber snout not five feet from the guy.   "Freeze!"   I hissed.

He had just struck a match and was cupping his cigarette with the other hand.   He froze, chagrin written all over his face.

This wasn't The Death Angel.   He was local muscle. He had a shoulder holster, but no hope to get to it before I blew him away.   The match was still burning.

"Don't move, sucker."   Hate flashed through his eyes.   I wanted to defuse the situation if I could.

"You and I don't have a beef.   We're both doing a job, right?"   It took a second, but I got a reluctant nod.   The fire was close enough to warm his fingers.

"I think we can solve this little problem without having you die today.   What do you think?"   The fire was at his fingers and his eyes flickered toward the match, and he winced.

"Don't move," I whispered harshly.   He didn't, and the match put itself out between his smudged thumb and forefinger.

Despite Betsy looking him in the eye, he croaked, "You damn son...."

"Now, now—remember you don't have to die today, right?"

"What then, Shamus?"

"Put your hands behind your head and walk in here."   He rose carefully, glaring at me the whole time.   As he got in far enough to let the door close, I stuck the muzzle under his chin.   The unlit smoke jostled, and I could see the calculation in his eyes.

"You know you can't beat my trigger finger.   No matter what happens to you for screwing up this job, it'll be better than me blowing your head off."

I carefully reached under his coat and pulled out his gat, a Smith & Wesson 38-caliber Police Special.   "Cute!   A Police Special.   Get kicked off the Force, did ya?"   I stuck it carefully in my belt, keeping my pistol snugly under his chin.

"Now turn around slowly and face the door." Before he finished his turn, I brought Betsy down hard on the back of his head. He dropped like a stone, and I let him crumple on the floor. He didn't twitch. Rope and duct tape from the storage room would keep him out of my hair plenty long enough for me to do what I needed to do. After I trussed him up, I eased down the hall and slipped into my office, gathering up three days' accumulation of mail and locking the door behind me.

There were no checks and nothing else of importance in the mail, so I dumped it on Chiquita's desk and went into my office, locking my private door as well.

The girl at Rose's office answered the line promptly and called for her. When she picked up, she sounded tense.

"It's me, Rose. Everything OK?"

"It's chilly enough for a fur coat, with Chiquita being my shadow. I told you she didn't like me."

"Yeah, Babe, but nobody has bothered you, have they?"

"No."

"Well, it's only a day and a half till the hearing. You're due at the lawyer's at 2:00 PM tomorrow afternoon to work on your testimony. I promised Greenberg we'd get you there safely and get you to the hearing looking good. I need to talk to Chiquita. Is she around?"

"Of course. She says it is orders to stay within touching distance. She didn't like it when I said touching distance was reserved for you. She's making a face at me now. Here she is."

I heard some movement, the phone clattering on the desk, it being picked up, and then a quiet, "Hello, Boss." Before I could speak, she continued. "Things pretty tense, Boss. Rose, she complains about me, but I know it's mostly worry about her case. I slept on the sofa last night, but I heard her crying in her bedroom."

"Chiquita, did you go anywhere between work and her flat?"

"No. I took her straight to her flat, then went out for submarines and made sure nobody followed." Her voice dropped furtively.

"Just the same, Boss, I got bad feelings out there. So I go back all around the block. No tail. But I still have bad feelings. This morning, Rose was real quiet. She didn't say much, and the trip to work wasn't bad. Not many people are out that early. We went one stop past her subway stop and walked back. I'm sure we weren't followed, but...."

"What did you do about lunch?"

"We brought some sandwiches from her place, so we didn't have to go out."

"Not at all?"

"The girls get a fifteen minute break in the morning and one in the afternoon. There's a little courtyard in the back where they go to smoke and gossip and eat lunch if the weather's good. Here's the problem: they all know what Rose is up to. She can't keep her mouth shut. They know about you, the hearing Friday, and what's at stake. I'm worried about getting her to that lawyer's office, Boss."

"Me too, Chick. I'm going to tail you escorting her to Greenberg's tomorrow. Don't say anything to her about me, just be careful.

"Manny's snitch says they've got flyers on me all over town. Pat says there's been a new face staking out his place the last couple of days. I'm calling you from the office and had to deal with a lookout in the hall. I'm not staying in the apartment, but hiding out in Midtown at a hotel near Carl's garage. And Chick, I've got the girl."

"What?!" she exploded.

I briefed her on last night's escapade.

"Why didn't you tell me what you were planning? And how do you know you got the right girl? You could've gotten killed, and it's still trespassing, and maybe kidnapping. That was crazy!" Thank goodness she cupped her hand around the mouthpiece.

"Hold on, hold on. When I went out to Menaphy's the second time—after I got beat up—I saw the girls playing on the lawn, and one looks just like a teenage Rose would look. She's the right age. She came from The Home. Her name is Angela, because Menaphy changed it from Angel. It's

135

gotta be her, Chiquita! And if I'm right, it's a damn good thing I got her out. If I'm wrong, we can still nail him for child abuse and child prostitution based on what she told me."

There was a long pause while she took it all in. "Well, that means I'll be babysitting Rose for sure, and all I can tell her is that you're hiding out too."

"Right, Kiddo. You've got your wish about me not seeing our favorite client. On the other hand, I'm not real comfortable babysitting a sixteen-year-old girl."

"Where do you have her?"

"I've got her holed up with me at the hotel. Carl's checking on her while I'm out."

"Does she have clothes?"

"Not much. She grabbed some, but we'd been discovered and didn't have any time."

"What about personal things?"

"What personal things?"

"*Personal* things, Boss."

"She has a little handbag, but I don't know what's in it. Listen, it's not like we're going anywhere...."

"Boss, a girl needs her things, period! You tell her I'll talk to her later today and arrange to get anything she needs. You hear me?"

"Yeah, I'll try to call again right before you leave for the day. Remember, mum's the word with Rose till after the hearing."

"I'll remember. It's not like we chitchat a lot. When do you want us to leave for Greenberg's office tomorrow?"

"At 1:00 PM. Call a cab to pick you up...don't flag one down. I'll be in a taxi down the block and tail you all the way to Greenberg's. When you get there, tell the receptionist...her name is Maureen...that you're my assistant and go with Rose all the way to his private office."

"Maureen? You're on a first name basis with her?"

"Good to know you're paying attention, Girl Friday! See ya tomorrow."

Alias Baby Girl

I dialed the Precinct. Steve was there, but on another line. I held till until I thought my ear would fall off. He finally picked up.

"Steve, things are really getting tight. Chiquita and I are taking Rose to Greenberg's tomorrow afternoon to work on her testimony. Rose has been with her two days and has the feeling they're being watched, but hasn't spotted anybody. Any word from the cops uptown on the judge's hit and run?"

"Casey, having you for a friend is like a scratchy label in the shirt collar. I like the shirt, but there's a lot of irritation involved. Where were you last night?"

"Why, Steve? Things not going well at home and you're hunting a date?"

"Casey, there's a limit to what I can do and what I want to do to keep your worthless hide out of trouble. Were you out on Long Island?"

"Why? What have you heard?"

"It's what I haven't heard that bothers me. I've gotten a funny phone call or two from the Commissioner's Office directing me to keep my ears open for any talk about break-ins and the like, despite the fact that Long Island is not remotely our jurisdiction. Early this morning a couple of Menaphy's security guards were getting buckshot removed at one of the local hospitals. What do you know about that?"

"Steve, you know I don't own any long guns. Was it a break-in? That place has more art than the Guggenheim. Keep me posted on anything you hear about it. Anyway, I'm laying low until this court hearing is over. Now, back to my original question, my irritable friend. Anything on the hit and run?"

"No, and there's not likely to be, and you know it."

"Just checking. Talk to you later." Steve knew it was me and wanted to know what was up, but not enough to really grill me. I could get away with stuff he only wished he could do.

I figured I'd better see if there was any word on Joey and Sam. Barnegat Police answered promptly and cousin Jack was jovial.

137

"So, Casey, Jersey is used to getting New York's garbage, but this is overdoing it. Two punks come down, rent a beach cabin but never take off a hat or a coat. Seriously, cousin, they got here almost before you called me. You want I should run 'em in for something?"

"Naw, just keep an eye on them and let me know if they check out of the motel. And if you can't get me, call Captain Butler at Greenwich Village Precinct."

"OK. What's up anyway?"

"Too long a story for right now, but a young girl's life is in jeopardy. I'll fill you in, hopefully, in a couple of days. Maybe I'll give myself a long weekend down there."

"Do it. I told Mom you'd called, and she said you were overdue by a couple of years and maybe you'd gotten too fancy for the family and were ashamed...."

"OK, OK, I get it. Tell your mother that I'll be down after this case, but only if she'll cook that apple cobbler she always made when we were kids. Those were good times. But this is serious business, Jack. Those two creeps are dangerous as cornered snakes. Treat 'em with care, Cousin."

It gave me a lift just thinking about those boyhood days, but a look at the clock brought me back quick. I carefully let myself out of the office and checked on my trussed-up thug who was beginning to stir and took off down the back stairs. It would take him a couple of hours to get free, and he wouldn't be eager to check in with his story anyway. He might not tell it at all.

I ducked into the garage and Carl said, Girl barely got her head out of the magazines to answer the door when I checked on her 'bout an hour ago."

"Thanks, Buddy. We've just got to sit tight for the next 36 hours."

Chapter 28

My cabbie was an old Brooklyn guy named Rocco who liked the idea of playing detective. He especially liked the fifty I gave him. We cruised the block before the girls' cab got there and nothing seemed out of line.

We were sitting a block away when Rose and Chiquita got in their cab promptly at 1:00 PM. My guy was good at discreetly tailing the girls, and we were half-way to Greenberg's office when he said, "Pal, I think we ain't the only ones in this poker game. We got a left turn coming up. If that navy Mercury behind us follows, we've got company, but I don't think they know we're playing too."

The Merc turned the corner with us, but I couldn't get a look at the two guys using our mirrors.

"Good work. Let 'em pass, Rocco. I need to ID these guys."

He flipped on his blinker, touched his brakes and headed toward the curb. I caught a glimpse as they passed, intent on Rose's cab, ignoring us completely. I didn't recognize 'em, but I would the next time I saw them.

"Be careful, but keep 'em in sight, Rocco," I said as I un-holstered Betsy, checked the clip and chambered a round.

My cabbie watched intently then said, "You really did mean to be careful, didn't ja?" After a moment, he said, "I'm figuring you for the good guy in this caper, or I'd drop you right here like a hot potato."

"I am one of the good guys this time. There've been a couple of shootings in this mess, and I don't think they'd try anything on Fifth Avenue, but those two girls are in danger. Stick close, even if it means they make us."

We were almost to Greenberg's building and the streets were full of vehicles and pedestrians. Nothing was going to happen here. The girls' cab and the Merc pulled over to the curb, and so did we a half a block back. Rose and Chiquita got out, and briskly entered the building.

The passenger quickly got out of the Merc, checked the area and followed the girls. I was fifty feet behind with a New York Post folded over Betsy. By the time he pushed through the brass revolving door, I was a couple of steps behind.

I entered the lobby as he was scanning the three elevators. The doors were closing on the far one and the two closer ones were still coming down. He was good. Without appearing to look around, he casually stepped to the back wall and lit a cigarette next to the standing ashtray, all the while eyeing the rising indicator on the third elevator. It stopped briefly on the second floor. By then, the doors on the second elevator were open, and I had to get on or mark myself as a tail. I couldn't see if the one carrying the girls stopped again before Greenberg's sixth floor.

That's OK, I thought. Nosey will have to check out at least one floor, and I'll be up there in time to get the girls out of the reception room before he arrives. I was alone on my car and the instant the doors opened on six, I bounded over to those massive doors and was inside in an instant. Chiquita and Rose were just starting toward the sofa. "Don't sit! Come with me." Startled, they paused, and I grabbed each by an elbow and pulled them toward the hall to the coffee room.

Maureen watched wide-eyed over the countertop. In a low voice, I said, "Gotta get them out of sight, and you have to deal with a guy in a brown suit that's coming through that door any second. You haven't seen two broads all day. Get it?"

She nodded as I hustled the girls down the hall and into the room. Chiquita whispered, "We got a tail, Boss?"

"Followed you all the way from Rose's work."

Rose's face was white, but her voice was steady. "Who is it?"

"Don't know, Rose, but it can't be good...shush!" We could hear the big door softly open and click shut. A man spoke to Maureen. "Pardon me, ma'am. I've seemed to have lost my wife and her girlfriend," he said with a little laugh. "I was supposed to meet them at an attorney's office in this building, and I've completely forgotten which one."

"Two women?" Maureen played it just right. "Well, it isn't this office. We haven't had any female clients all day. If you'd like to leave your name and number..."

"No, thanks, I'll find 'em." A few moments after the door latch clicked, Maureen's heels clicked along the hallway toward us. She glanced toward the front before speaking low and rapidly.

"Brown suit, dull yellow patterned tie, tall as you Casey, a little heavier, funny eyes...one brown and one gray. Spoke friendly, but his eyes were hard, scary. Know him?"

"No, but remember him Maureen. Call me if you ever see him again. I'll brief David on this. He's expecting us at 2:00...or at least Rose and Chiquita. Did you get a chance to tell him they were here?"

"No. You busted in as I was dialing his extension. I'll call now."

"Not from out front, Maureen. Go tell him or use another phone."

"Sure, Casey. Wait here."

Since the coffeepot was there, I poured a cup for Rose who took it silently and added cream and sugar. Chiquita waved off a cup with a worried look. I took mine black, like my mood. I think we just met The Death Angel.

Chapter 29

Maureen was back in a moment. "Come this way," she said, leading us down the hall.

David was holding his door open and greeted Rose warmly, shook hands with Chiquita as I introduced her, and waved her and me toward the sofa. As he guided Rose toward the seat in front of his desk, he asked me. "What was that all about?"

I quickly told him about the cab ride and my suspicion that the tail was using Rose to find me. "We dodged him on the way in, but I'm sure he'll be watching for the girls to leave. I don't think he saw my face or connected me with them, but he'll put two and two together if he sees me again."

David listened intently, elbows on his chair arms, fingers tented and touching his lips. "We can handle that, Mr. Stone. We have an office in the adjoining building with private access through the second level basement. You will be able to leave by an entirely different route. As you might guess, we have had many occasions where our clients required absolute confidentiality, and we have found it advantageous to have a secret office."

Rose visibly relaxed. Turning to her, David said with a reassuring smile, "Now, young lady, let's prepare for court."

Chiquita and I moved to the sofa in a far corner, and she leaned over to whisper, "What do we do now, Boss? They followed us from work, and you know they're watching her apartment too."

"Yeah, you're right. We can get out of here on the sly, but we need to disappear until the hearing tomorrow. I'll be OK at the hotel, but I can't take you and Rose there because of the girl. They can't meet until we're sure she's the right girl. Do you think you could hide Rose out at Tia's? I'll pay whatever she says to cover the cost."

"I'll call," she said quietly, slipping out of the room.

My attention turned to Rose and Lawyer Greenberg. It was soon apparent that he had earned this fancy office. He was good: posing questions, listening carefully, gently interrupting to clarify a point, focusing her responses on the crucial issues. I watched, fascinated as her tense, tentative demeanor became relaxed and confident, and her answers clear and responsive.

Chiquita returned quietly and whispered that Tia would be happy to have Rose overnight, and we settled back watching David and Rose work. After a half hour, David pushed back from his desk. "Let's take a break. Then we'll try a little cross-examination, with emphasis on the 'cross,'" he said with a smile.

As we all stood, he spoke into his intercom requesting refreshments. I shared our newly made overnight plans and both David and Rose nodded approval. Rose stretched and stepped toward the large windows overlooking Fifth Avenue.

"No! Not the windows, Rose." She jumped at my voice. "Don't take the chance. They know you're in the building and had a good look at you earlier."

"Sure, Casey, I didn't even think...."

"No harm done. It's just that we can't be too careful. Sorry I startled you."

Maureen appeared just then after a rap on the door, carrying a tray of coffee and soft drinks. She asked the girls what they wanted and while passing out their drinks, David motioned me to his credenza on the far side of the office.

"You're pretty uptight about all this, Stone."

"You'd better believe it, David. The Mob has a contract on me and pulled in a guy from Chicago to do the job. I doubt it will stay just a job on me if tomorrow's hearing goes well. Sooner or later Joey and Menaphy are going to figure this out and join forces. Menaphy's security is Mob…onnected, and they got roughed up night before last. One of them is the brother of Joey's bodyguard. Nobody connected with this case is happy today."

"I have a license for my handgun, Stone. Should I take it to court in the morning?"

"Thanks, Counselor, but no thanks! It's a closed hearing. I'll be there, and Chiquita will be too, right behind Rose until she takes the witness stand. Both of us will be armed. Just get us in without being frisked and we're OK. Besides, when was the last time you fired a handgun at a person?"

"Ahhhh," he said with a small nod. "I take your point. I'll stick to the pen and count on it being mightier than the sword."

Maureen appeared between us and handed David a coffee well creamed and sugared, then turning to me, said in a sultry voice, "I know just how you like it too."

"Oh my," murmured David with a smile, turning back toward his desk as she handed me a steaming mug of black coffee.

Continuing across the room, he said, "OK, back to work. Miss Kelly." Rose took her seat intent on his instruction.

"Cross-examination is intended to show inconsistencies in your testimony, gaps in your knowledge, whittle away at your certainties and leave the impression that you are not honest and forthcoming. The easiest way to combat that is to be completely honest. Answer as briefly and directly as you can. Don't volunteer anything—just say enough to accurately answer. The right answer may be that you don't know or you don't remember. The judge has seen thousands of witnesses. He'll know if you're being honest.

"Now, I'm going to play the other attorney. I'm going to ask questions you may find impertinent, insulting, or inappropriate. Your job is to listen carefully, answer as briefly as possible, and not get mad. The instant you get mad, you become your own worst enemy."

As he questioned her, David's entire manner changed. By turns he was ingratiating, accusatory, disdainful, hostile, disbelieving. After an hour, Rose was limp, with a damp hanky where she dabbed away tears, but had earned a sincere, "well done!" from David.

"You'll do just fine tomorrow, Miss Kelly. Get a good night's sleep. Dress as you would for church, and I'll meet you at the Courthouse, Room 234 C, promptly at 8:45. This is a restricted hearing. To gain your admittance, I will identify you as a witness, Miss Rodriquez as a member of my staff, and Mr. Stone as an investigator for the firm to locate missing persons. See you tomorrow morning."

Maureen led us through a series of hallways, private elevators and passageways until we were back on the street in an entirely different area from where we had entered. Chiquita said they would get her proper clothes, and we agreed that the girls would take a cab to my hotel in the morning, and we would ride to court together. I felt good about things. Chiquita even took Rose's hand as they headed toward the subway.

Chapter 30

Friday morning came after a restless night. Angela was persistent, peppering me with endless questions about what was going to happen in court, what would happen to her, how long she had to stay cooped up, who, when, where, until I finally put my finger over her lips and said, "Shush!" She pouted for a moment, then laughingly jumped up and gave me a peck on the cheek.

"OK, Mr. Casey. Orange juice, bagel and some more magazines..."

I gave a dramatic sigh and loudly complained, "My whole life is run by bossy women."

She laughed again and pushed me out the door with the command, "... and hurry, I'm hungry!"

Carl had picked up my suit and laundry from the cleaners. I dressed with the care befitting the occasion: crisp shirt and a good silk tie. I carefully slipped on my shoulder holster not wrinkling the shirt. Betsy fit snugly in giving cool solid comfort. Nobody was getting to my client or me today. My coat had been tailored to fit over my .45 and there was no hint of Betsy as I buttoned up.

I gave myself the once over: face still bruised, but not too bad. I looked my best, which wasn't very good.

When the girls' cab arrived, I hopped in the front seat and turned to look them over. They were too tense to do more than nod. I needed to lighten the mood.

Chiquita was in a gray suit with a white blouse that had a frilly bow at the throat. Her outfit fairly screamed pricey law firm executive secretary despite accenting her ample curves everywhere you looked. "Really nice, Girl Friday! How come I never get this look at the office?" She stuck out her tongue and said, "Pay me better Boss man." We all three laughed and the cabbie guffawed.

Rose was lovely. Church clothes for her had meant a navy sheath with a modest scoop neck, yellow gold rope chain with a large teardrop opal pendant and matching earrings. Her blonde hair fell full on both sides of her face. Her eyes were lightly shadowed and lips highlighted with red. The blush on her cheeks was in response to my stare. Dark stockings flowed into navy suede pumps. Her matching purse had gold trim.

"Wow," was all I could get out. "Wow, Rose. Where'd you get all this?"

"Tia," they answered in unison. "It was like a pajama party," Rose giggled. "She had eight nieces and sisters come over, and they put it all together."

"She had to try on six pairs of heels before she got the right ones, though," Chiquita hooted. "Then the handbag...." The girls looked at each other and broke into giggles again, holding hands like schoolgirls. I couldn't believe the transformation of these two alley cats. I turned back to the front and our cabbie rolled his eyes as another wave of giggles swept over us.

The closer we got to the Courthouse, the quieter it got in our cab. Nervous giggles had disappeared.

"Two blocks, girls. Heads up." We rode the rest of the way in silence, eyeing the area carefully as the somber façade of the courthouse came into view. All the things that could go wrong flooded my mind. With a pang, I recalled my trial for being the winner in a shootout several years ago and the persistent heartburn of those days. Lady Justice saw through that blindfold and I was exonerated, but I still got tense any time I had to come back.

"All clear. Let's go." I paid the hack, and we hurried into the imposing building and walked up the marble staircase to the second floor balcony that overlooked the main lobby. David Greenberg, Esquire, looked every bit the part, in a slate gray suit with a faint pinstripe, white shirt with French cuffs, dark pewter silk tie held in place by a modest—but clearly real—diamond stickpin. His black leather briefcase bespoke quality as well as extensive use. He radiated calm and confidence.

As he shook my hand, he gazed with frank admiration at my companions. "Mr. Stone, you are indeed fortunate to be surrounded by such loveliness." When he took Rose's hand and lightly brought it to his lips, her cheeks flushed. He repeated the gesture with Chiquita, who rewarded him with a tiny curtsy.

He took a deep breath savoring the view before addressing us.

"I checked with the court clerk and with the late judge's personal secretary, Miss Fregossi. The judge is in his chambers. He has studied the pleadings and reviewed the file. He wants the attorneys, parties and witnesses in place when the bailiff opens court precisely at 9 o'clock. That gives us fifteen minutes.

"We have just enough time for a rest stop before court, always a good idea. Ladies, yours is down the hall to the left, and we'll be here waiting for you.

When they returned, David ushered our procession past the bailiff into the courtroom. It had a high ceiling with dark walnut paneling on the walls. The great seal of the State of New York hung behind the judge's chair, and a brass nameplate centered on the bench stated, "Hon. Jonathan Law."

Greenberg pushed through the gate at the bar and laid his briefcase on the counsel table to the right. He motioned Chiquita to a chair immediately behind him and Rose to the chair beside him at the table. I took a seat at the rear of the room where I could see everything.

Almost immediately we were followed by a small man carrying an alligator briefcase in a navy striped suit, a shocking red tie and alligator shoes. His black hair was slicked straight back and his eyes darted all over the courtroom as he strutted to the other counsel table. He was followed by an impeccably attired Joseph Menaphy, who joined him at the table without glancing right or left.

The small man spread a number of papers from his briefcase over the table, then turning to David, said rather imperiously, "Mr. Greenberg, I presume?" Without pausing for a response, he continued with, "I'm Snavely. We spoke by phone...."

David made him wait for a reply, straightening some papers on the table before extending his hand and saying, "Yes, of course. Nice to meet you in person, Mr. Snavely."

The little man shook hands reluctantly and asked, "Have you heard anything from the alternate beneficiary, Mr. Joey Catalano?"

"No, have you?"

"No, and I can't understand it. He should be vitally interested."

"Well," David said mildly, "everyone is required to protect their own interest, but his is utterly dependent on whether the primary beneficiary is located, don't you agree?"

Snavely grunted and sat down beside Mr. Menaphy who hadn't moved, staring straight ahead, hands folded in his lap.

Silence lay over the courtroom with the weight of a gathering storm. A clock high on the back wall of the courtroom ticked loudly. David whispered reassuringly to Rose whom I could see was getting tense.

Promptly as the clock indicated 9:00, the door behind the bench swung open and the bailiff stepped into the courtroom with the command, "All rise!"

With a flourish of black robe and white hair, a tall, cadaverous man swept through the door and up the three steps to his throne where he stood motionless, fixing his piercing black eyes on us. He was followed by Miss Fregossi who stood next to her chair and desk two steps below his.

The bailiff's voice rung out again with the centuries old call to order.

"Oh yez, oh yez, all persons having business with this honorable court come forth and give heed. God bless these United States, the great state of New York, and this honorable court, Amen."

The judge ceremoniously sat and the bailiff's voice rung out again, "Be seated and give your attention to the court." His Honor waited until the shuffle of feet and bodies had died to a complete silence. His voice was deep and riveting.

"Mr. Greenberg, are you ready to proceed?"

David rose and said, "We are, Your Honor."

The judge turned and said, "Mr. Snavely, are you ready to proceed?"

He sprang to his feet and piped, "We certainly are, Your Honor," looking at David.

Jonathan Law, Judge, waited, eyes fixed on Snavely until he returned the gaze. "Mr. Snavely, you will address your remarks to the court, unless otherwise instructed."

Snavely nodded and meekly said, "Yes, Your Honor."

The judge watched until Snavely was well settled in his seat, then turned and said, "Mr. Greenberg, your Petition raises questions of morality as well as legal sufficiency. What have you to offer that would persuade the court to overturn a legal act of sixteen years ago which would violate the privacy of several people by opening a sealed adoption file?" His voice was hard. His manner signified an intent to deal with this matter with dispatch.

David rose unhurriedly and met the judge's eyes and quietly said, "The mother."

His words hung in the air as the clock ticked. The judge leaned back, gaze fixed on David and said, "Put her on."

David patted Rose on the shoulder, pulled out her chair as she stood and pointed her to the witness stand. All eyes in the courtroom followed her walk to the front. She remained standing and raised her right hand as the bailiff administered the time—honored oath, "Do you swear to tell the truth, the whole truth, and nothing but the truth, so help you God?"

"I do." Her voice was clear and strong.

Attorney Greenberg started at the beginning, with her name and address, and seamlessly took her through her story, producing a certified copy of her birth certificate to confirm her tender age at the time she entered The Home. I unconsciously tensed as he neared the crucial part. David was standing at the podium and spoke softly without referring to his notes.

"Miss Kelly, you had just graduated from high school, correct?"

"Yes."

"Had you ever filled out a job application?"

"No."

"Had you ever applied for credit?"

"No."

"Had you ever signed a lease?"

"No."

"Did The Home give you a copy of the adoption papers when you started living there?"

"No."

"When did you first see the adoption papers before signing?"

"When they made me sign."

"Your Honor, may I have the Surrender document from the court's file?"

"Certainly, Mr. Greenberg." The judge shuffled through the file and handed him a three-page document covered with fine print. David handed it to Rose.

"Look at this carefully, particularly at the bottom of the last page." He gave her a few moments as she scanned the pages and finally settled on the last page, her face registering tearful sadness.

"Do you recognize the signature on the last page?"

"Yes."

"Whose is it?"

"Mine," she whispered.

"Where were you when you signed it?"

"In the delivery room in the basement of The Home."

"Where were you in the delivery room?"

"On the table."

"Who was there with you?"

"The doctor, the nurse and the matron with the papers."

"How long after the birth of your daughter was it?"

"They were still cleaning her on the table beside me. She was crying, so was I. They wouldn't even let me hold her to say goodbye."

Rose broke down, quietly sobbing into her handkerchief. Chiquita was sniffling. All the men in the room save the judge were shifting uneasily in their seats.

"Break, Mr. Greenberg?" the judge asked David.

"Two more questions, Your Honor."

The judge nodded and turned back to Rose who looked up at David, dabbing her eyes.

"What are the smudges on that page?"

"My tears."

"How old were you?"

"Two months past my seventeenth birthday."

"Thank you, Miss Kelly," David said quietly. Then addressing the judge, he said, "We pass the witness for cross-examination, Your Honor, but would like a brief recess."

"Fifteen minutes," the judge said striking his gavel on the pad a bit more strongly than needed.

Rose descended from the witness box to be enveloped in Chiquita's arms. Menaphy stood and turned, his face registering shock as he spotted me. He grabbed Snavely's arm and they were still in deep conversation as our side exited to the rear of the courtroom.

"Oh, Rose," blubbered Chiquita, arm around her waist, "You were wonderful!"

David seconded the congratulations as he let the courtroom door shut behind them.

"You're doing perfectly, Rose. Now, take a break. Mr. Snavely will begin cross-examination when we return."

Chapter 31

We did not encounter Snavely, Menaphy or any strangers in the hall. Upon our return, Menaphy was seated stiffly at the counsel table, eyes straightforward, just as before. The bailiff preceded the judge into the courtroom from his chambers announcing, "Court is back in session."

The judge leaned toward Rose and almost kindly said, "Young lady, you're still under oath." She gave a wan smile and a little nod.

Turning forward, the judge said, "You may proceed, Mr. Snavely, but be advised that the Court is primarily interested in the adequacy of a Surrender executed by a minor, without legal or parental advice, under circumstances of extreme stress."

The judge got it! I smiled to myself and relaxed a bit on the back bench.

Snavely wasn't stupid. He questioned Rose gently but firmly.

"Miss Kelly, you weren't married at the time you became pregnant...?" He emphasized the "Miss" which drew a glare from Rose as she answered.

"That's correct."

"And the father wouldn't marry you, correct?"

"Yes."

"In fact, he ran off to whereabouts unknown..."

"Yes," she said through clinched teeth.

"And didn't contact you ever thereafter?"

"That's right."

"Let me see if I understand your situation then. You were unmarried, pregnant, the father ran off, you had no job, no money, and were on the street without a home?"

"Yes," she hissed.

"It must have been frightening, even terrifying for a young girl," Snavely said with feigned sympathy.

"It was." Rose relaxed a little, and I tensed a little.

"And then you saw a notice in Grand Central Station about The Home, didn't you?"

"Yes, I did."

"It was a ray of hope in a seemingly hopeless situation, wasn't it?"

"Yes." She nodded vigorously.

"And you walked twenty blocks across town to seek them out, right?"

"Yes."

"When you got there, they made you stay in the lobby until you had read and decided to enter into the Entrance Agreement?"

"That's correct."

"Let's look at that Agreement together, shall we? Your Honor, may I approach the witness?" Snavely got and handed her the Agreement.

"Miss Kelly, please examine this document. You do read, don't you?"

Her head snapped up, eyes flashing. A retort was half out of her mouth when David dropped his pen on the floor and loudly scooted his chair back to retrieve it. She froze. David sat back up, rather red-faced, and apologetic. "Sorry, Your Honor."

"Hummm," the judge said, then turning to Rose, instructed, "Answer the question, Miss Kelly."

By then, Rose had recovered her composure and said, "Yes, I can read it Mr. Snavely. What can I help you understand?"

He colored slightly and demanded, "Read aloud the bold face sentence at the top of page one."

Rose enunciated clearly. *"Notice: This is a legally binding agreement."*

"And Miss Kelly, at the bottom of page 2. Please read us that bold face statement."

As she flipped the page over, I saw her spunk waning. *"Notice: Do not sign this document until you have read and understood it and intend to be bound hereby."*

"One last sentence, Miss Kelly," pointing to the bottom of the page.

She read quietly. "In return for The Home providing room and board and medical supervision throughout your pregnancy and delivery, without cost, I, the undersigned, agree to surrender my baby(ies) for adoption."

"Now, Miss Kelly. Did you have any question about what that statement meant?"

Her head was down and her voice was low, as she answered, "No."

"Is that your signature right below the statement?"

"Yes," she whispered.

"Sorry, I didn't hear you. Would you speak up please?"

"Yes," she spit through gritted teeth.

Snavely turned to his seat with a little smile and said, "Thank you, Miss Kelly. That will be all."

When Snavely sat down, the judge turned from Rose to David and with raised eyebrows asked, "Redirect, Counselor, or recess?"

"Only a couple of questions, may it please the Court."

The judge nodded imperceptibly and replied, "Try your case as you will."

David remained standing at the counsel table and briefly re-emphasized her tender years and the physical and mental stress of the signing in the delivery room.

When he finished, the judge asked, "Next witness, Mr. Greenberg?"

"Not at this time, Your Honor. If, however, you should sustain our Petition to Open the File, we certainly will have further questions based on the contents thereof."

"Yes, of course. Mr. Snavely, put on your first witness."

Snavely stood and said, "We call Mr. Joseph K. Menaphy to the stand."

Menaphy walked briskly to the stand without glancing our way and took the oath with a firm, "I do." He sat and calmly answered all the background questions posed by his attorney to establish his identity, standing in the community and record of community service. Snavely finally got to the good stuff.

"What connection do you have with The Home, Mr. Menaphy?"

"It has been my favorite charity for over twenty years. I have contributed directly to it. I have hosted fundraising events. I have served on the Board of Directors as member and chairman."

"As a Board member, what concerns have you dealt with?"

"Keeping the institution on a sound financial basis is essential...otherwise, we cannot continue to serve the pressing need of young girls with unexpected and unwanted pregnancies. We face maintenance of our physical plant, staffing needs, room and board for our girls, and most importantly, the medical supervision throughout pregnancy and delivery. We take our responsibilities most seriously."

"What provision do you make for the babies, Mr. Menaphy?"

"Over the years, we carefully have built a reputation for healthy babies available for problem-free adoptions. With complete confidentiality!" He emphasized.

"What steps do you take to ensure confidentiality?"

"No girl is admitted to our facility without a thorough explanation of our policies and a written acknowledgment of that explanation and their understanding and acceptance of it. There is no ambiguity on this point, and the girls ordinarily are quite grateful. As you might imagine, they are often ashamed, embarrassed and humiliated. Typically, families are shocked...even horrified...at the pregnancy, and confidentiality is not only welcome, but essential."

"How do adopting parents feel about this?"

Mr. Menaphy leaned forward in the witness stand and tapped his finger with each word. "Just as strongly as the girls do." He straightened. "Mr. Snavely, if we could not guarantee absolute confidentiality, we would never be able to place a child. Our organization would collapse virtually overnight. That's why the mother's Surrender form emphasizes the complete termination of maternal and legal bonds and the impossibility of establishing contact at a later date."

Snavely asked for the Entrance and Surrender forms from the file, and the Judge complied. Reviewing them, Menaphy pointed out the bold-faced type confirming confidentiality and the finality of the surrender and added, "We have been extremely careful to do everything in a proper and legal manner." Turning to the judge, he continued, "Your Honor, our institution was established decades ago by a lawyer, whose heart was torn by the plight of so many girls right here in our city who might otherwise be left to the unscrupulous, the back alley abortionists, or abandoned on the streets. We take our mission seriously and confidentiality is at its heart."

Snavely asked Menaphy to confirm that Rose's signature was on all the papers in the proper place then sat down with the statement to Mr. Greenberg, "You may ask."

David stood and walked thoughtfully to the podium. "You understand that Rose Kelly was a minor at the time she signed those documents, don't you?"

Menaphy shifted in his seat before responding. "Well, I heard her testify to that a while ago."

"And her birth certificate was introduced confirming the accuracy of her statements....?"

Menaphy shifted again and grudgingly conceded, "Yes."

"Mr. Menaphy, The Home simply took advantage of Rose Kelly's tender years and extreme circumstances, did it not?"

"No! I am sure they did not. Although I was not present at the time, we are very careful about such things. If she had parents, we would have gotten their permission. Of course, if she told the staff she was an orphan...." He let that possibility hang in the air, and the judge's eyebrows went up as he glanced at Mr. Snavely, then at Mr. Greenberg.

"You have no reason to believe that is the case, do you, Mr. Menaphy?" I heard a bit of tension in David's voice.

"Well, yes, I do, Mr. Greenberg. I reviewed The Home's file before trial and there's a staff notation to that effect."

"I'd like to see that document, please."

"Certainly, Mr. Greenberg. Mr. Snavely has the file."

As Snavely passed the file to the bailiff to hand to Mr. Menaphy, David turned to the table to get his yellow pad and glanced at me with raised eyebrows. I gave a little shrug. There was nothing like that in the material that Chiquita brought me. As David turned back to the podium, Chick looked back and gave me the same shrug I had just given David.

"Ah, here it is," Menaphy said pulling a note from the file. "Applicant says she is an orphan, father having died in Germany in the war; mother of tuberculosis."

"May I see that, please?" David stepped toward the witness stand, took the note, and returned to the counsel table where he and Rose leaned over it whispering.

Returning to the podium, he asked, "It appears to be undated..."

"Yes."

"... and unsigned."

"Yes."

"The handwriting is very distinctive. Do you recognize it?"

Mr. Menaphy held the note, and hesitated. I knew it wasn't in the copies Chiquita brought me.

"It appears to be written by our Head Matron, Miss Kathy Jones."

"Thank you, Mr. Menaphy."

The judge rapped his gavel and said, "Lunch. Court will reconvene at 1:30." We all stood as the judge arose, and he and Miss Fregossi disappeared into his chambers. David waved me to the table as Snavely and Mr. Menaphy left.

When we were alone, Chiquita blurted, "There was no such note when I saw the file"

"You saw the file?" David said.

Alias Baby Girl

Before she could answer, Rose cleared her throat. "Don't worry, Mr. Greenberg, just put me on the stand when we come back." I couldn't believe her grin.

Chapter 32

We spent the lunch break in the Jury Room. A clerk from David's office brought us sandwiches and drinks. As we ate, I used the court's phone and called the Greenwich Precinct. When Steve picked up, he skipped the hellos.

"How's it going Casey?"

"Can't tell yet. Right before lunch, Menaphy threw us a curve ball. He produced a note from the file, claiming Rose told them she was an orphan and, therefore, her signature would be adequate. Rose will take the stand after lunch to try to refute it."

"Let us know as things happen. Remember, we have uniforms and a detective waiting to move on The Home at your signal and the police on Long Island are just waiting for my go ahead to enter Menaphy's estate. Now listen up. Your cousin in Barnegat called me about an hour and a half ago. Joey and Sam suddenly threw their bags in the car and took off, headed toward Manhattan, burning rubber."

"The judge's secretary! She must have called during morning break. Any other bad news?"

"Our people on the street hear a constant patter of 'Angel of Death is in town'. You be careful, Casey, and watch out for Rose too. Judge's secretary is probably savvy enough to know your client is going to take the stand again, and ..."

There was a sharp rap on the door.

"Got it, Steve. I'll be in touch."

The bailiff stuck his head in through the doorway. "Twenty minutes till court resumes. Is one of you Casey Stone?"

"Me. Why?"

"Note for you," he said, handing me a small envelope.

"Where did it come from?"

"Some man dropped it off with one of the court clerks and said you were in the trial before Judge Law."

Chiquita looked over my shoulder as I tore open the envelope. It was our mystery friend—same paper, same typewriter, terse message.

> If the judge opens the file, he also opens Pandora's box. The Angel is on your tail and knows about the trial. Rose is in danger and so are you and your assistant. Careful when you leave.

I passed the note to David who scanned it and passed it wordlessly to Rose. We sat looking at each other for a moment before David broke the silence.

"Is this the same sender as before, Casey?"

"Looks like it."

"He knows a lot."

"Yeah."

"This Angel business is distressing. Mr. Stone, I can't spirit us out of the courthouse as we did at my office. Any thoughts?"

I called Steve again and quickly got the promise of a couple of plainclothes officers.

As I hung up, the bailiff knocked on the door. "Time for court."

When the judge was seated, Snavely said he had no further witnesses, and the judge turned to Mr. Greenberg. "Rebuttal, Counselor?"

"Yes, Your Honor. We recall Miss Kelly to the stand."

When she was seated, David asked, "How many years ago were you a resident at The Home?"

"Sixteen."

"Who was the Head Matron at that time?"

"Mildred Williams."

"Not Kathy Jones?"

"There was nobody by that name there sixteen years ago."

"How long did you live at The Home?"

"Almost six months."

"During that period of time, did you become familiar with the handwriting of Mildred Williams, the Head Matron?"

"I saw her handwriting a dozen times a day. She wrote the daily assignments for each girl and wrote the notices for the Bulletin Board and various other things."

David got the note from Mr. Snavely who surrendered it reluctantly, and laid it in front of Rose.

"Please look carefully at this and tell the court if you recognize the handwriting."

Rose studied it for only a moment, looked at the judge, and said, "I've never seen this handwriting before. It is not the handwriting of Mildred Williams, the Head Matron when I was there."

The judge leaned sharply forward, his anger obvious.

"Mr. Snavely, who has had custody of these records?"

"Well," Snavely stammered, rising to his feet, "they are kept at The Home as a regular part of their business records." He looked at Mr. Menaphy, seeking confirmation and received a curt nod.

"Who is personally in charge of them?" The tension was palpable.

Snavely bent over and whispered to Menaphy then replied, "Kathy Jones, the Head Matron. They are kept locked in her office."

The judge's parchment countenance was coloring and his next question was directly to Mr. Menaphy. "Sir, how long has Miss Kathy Jones been Head Matron?"

"Five years, Your Honor," he answered stiffly.

"The events we are concerned with occurred sixteen years ago!" The judge's voice rose to a roar. "Where did that note come from?"

Alias Baby Girl

"I'm afraid I can't say, Your Honor." Menaphy was getting a little green.

"Gentlemen," the judge spoke in measured tones, "The Court rules that the adoption file shall be opened. We will be in recess for one-half hour. The two attorneys will examine the file in my chambers, together, in the presence of the bailiff. When we return, Mr. Greenberg may reopen his case. In the meantime, Mr. Snavely, your clients are in contempt of court and the consequences depend on what happens throughout the balance of this trial." The gavel banged. "We are in recess. Lawyers, follow me."

Miss Fregossi fluttered to the door and held it for the judge, who stalked through, followed quickly by Esquires Greenberg and Snavely and the bailiff. When it slammed shut, Rose, Chiquita, and I were left alone with a visibly uncomfortable Joseph K. Menaphy. He stood and turned to me.

"Mr. Stone, may I speak to you privately?"

I indicated the rear door with a nod. When we were in the hall, he spoke in a low voice.

"Exactly how are you involved in this matter, Mr. Stone?"

"I do investigative work for Greenberg's firm. Remember, they were the ones that got me the introduction to you. I've been hired to find the girl."

He paused, calculation visible in his eyes. "This matter of confidentiality is paramount for The Home. It would be worth a lot...a lot, Mr. Stone...to The Home if that confidentiality were preserved for the girl and the adopting parties."

"I understand, Mr. Menaphy, but I'd be finished in this town if I didn't honor a deal."

"I appreciate your loyalty, Mr. Stone." He leaned close. "When I said, 'a lot,' I meant you'd never have to work again."

Before I could answer, Rose and Chiquita pushed through the door and Menaphy and I each stepped back with a start. The girls walked quickly between us and down the hall to the right. I watched them carefully all the way until they entered the restroom. As the door closed behind them, I heard two sets of footsteps behind me coming up the stairs from the lobby accompanied by two voices.

"This is it. Look for the courtroom."

"Right, Boss."

It was Joey and Sam. As they appeared in the stairwell only twenty feet away, our eyes locked.

"Hi, boys. Come to make good on your parking tickets?"

Chapter 33

The instant Joey and Sam reached the top step, I saw a flash at the far end of the balcony just over Menaphy's shoulder. At the same time I heard a sharp crack as the slug hit the marble wall behind me. Menaphy froze, staring at the pockmark, mouth agape. Joey jumped and stumbled back down the steps, grabbing at the railing. Sam dropped to a crouch, fanning his pistol out from under his coat.

I ducked into the recessed entrance to the courtroom door and scanned the balcony, but didn't draw my gun. Nothing moved but the Ladies' restroom door.

"No, Chick! Lock the door!"

Shouts and footsteps flooded up the stairs and two panting uniformed court guards arrived with guns drawn. They leveled them at Sam and both shouted, "Drop it!"

It really hurt to do it, but I yelled at them, "Not him! Down there!" pointing at the far end of the balcony.

One officer ran along the balcony as the other took Sam's gun before following his partner. I watched as they slowed and searched, knowing that The Angel wouldn't be there. Ignoring Menaphy who hadn't moved, and Sam who had regained his feet, I walked after the officers until I came to the restroom door and rapped on it, giving the girls the OK. I whispered as they emerged.

"He's long gone, but it had to be The Death Angel. I didn't see anything but the flash of his gun. Joey and Sam showed up just as he shot."

Rose paled. "Joey and Sam are here?"

165

"Yeah, Babe."

"Will they be in the courtroom?"

"Joey has a right to be there, and I'm sure they'll let Sam in under the circumstances, but the guards took his gun."

"I'm scared, Casey."

"Chiquita and I will be there and remember, Captain Butler's sending two plainclothes officers."

The hubbub back at the courtroom was caused by the courtroom cops, a collection of clerks, the reporters with flashbulbs popping and our two officers. One of the plainclothesmen spotted me and led the two of them over.

"Stone, isn't it?"

"Yeah."

"This is Detective Brown. I'm Miller. I worked that shooting at your place."

"Thanks." I wanted to get off that subject quick. "Here's the deal. The shooter was after me. We're about ready to go back into court." I gave a nod toward Joey and Sam. "Those two would love to rub us out, but wouldn't do it here, even if the goon had his gun.

"You know I'm carrying, but my girl is too. She's probably a better shot than you or me. Show him your license, Chiquita."

"No need. Captain Butler OK'd you. Got any description of the shooter?"

"You won't find him, but he's my size and age, a little heavier, and has one blue and one brown eye. Talks kind of flat."

The bailiff appeared at the courtroom door. "All persons authorized to attend Judge Law's hearing, please report to the courtroom."

Menaphy was still at the door, and the bailiff's call broke his trance. The girls and I followed him with Brown and Miller on our heels, after showing their IDs and a brief talk with the bailiff. Joey and Sam made it in too after considerable discussion with the bailiff. The bailiff pointed Joey to a seat inside the bar near Menaphy's table and then stepped briskly to the judge's door after locking the courtroom. As soon as he touched the handle, Judge Law strode in followed by the two lawyers and Miss Fregossi.

His Honor didn't wait for the bailiff. "Everyone be seated." As he surveyed the courtroom, the judge asked, "New people, Mr. Bailiff?"

"Yes, sir. Two city police as a result of the disturbance in the hall, and this is Joey Catalano, the alternate trust beneficiary. The other gentleman is his associate, Sam Napolitano."

The judge nodded his understanding, then said, "Is the courtroom secure?"

Yes, Your Honor," the bailiff responded.
"Then let us proceed. Mr. Greenberg?"

"We recall Mr. Menaphy to the stand, Your Honor."

The judge looked at Menaphy as he approached the stand and said, "Sir, you are still under oath."

Menaphy approached the witness stand like it was the electric chair. Snavely was nervously twirling a pencil. Greenberg had the look of a wolf closing in for the kill.

"The child in question, Miss Kelly's infant, was taken by you, wasn't she?"

Menaphy mumbled, cleared his throat, and said, "Yes."

"What name did you give her?"

"Angela."

"Where is she now?"

Menaphy looked up. "She has lived on my estate all her life. Two nights ago, she ran away."

"Ran away? Has she ever done so before?"

"No, my estate is walled and gated. The girls can't...." He interrupted himself, and the judge snapped his chair forward.

"Finish that sentence, Mr. Menaphy."

Menaphy's eyes shot over to Snavely, who busied himself taking notes.

"Mr. Menaphy...!"

With a tremor in his voice, Menaphy continued. "The girls are not permitted out of their housing, or the estate at night."

David jumped in. "Girls! How many girls!"

"Twelve."

"Twelve?!   Where did they come from?"

The silence was so deep I could hear my heart beat.

"Answer the question."   The judge's pale countenance reddened.

"The Home."

"All of them?"   Asked David.

"Yes."   Came the whisper.

"What are their ages?"

"Eight to sixteen...."

"Names and birthdates, Mr. Menaphy," the judge demanded.   "Miss Fregossi, take this down."   After Menaphy finished, the judge said, "Miss Fregossi, pull the files on each girl and bring them to the bench."   As she left, he turned to David and said, "Continue, Mr. Greenberg."

"Why would Angela run away?"

"I don't know."

"Tell us what you do know about her running away."

"Nothing.   She simply was not there at the wake-up call or anywhere on the grounds."

"Did you report it to the police?"

"No, I thought she'd come back."

"Mr. Menaphy, your oath requires the whole truth.   Two of your guards required medical attention for buckshot wounds that night.   Is that correct?"

"Yes, an unfortunate accident testing a new gun."

"Nothing to do with Angela running away?"

"Certainly not."

"Who is the pediatrician for the girls?"

"Dr. Reuben Semansky."

"Where is he located?"

"Just a couple of miles from my home, but he comes to the estate to examine the girls."

"How long has Dr. Semansky tended Angela?"

"From infancy."

"Has she seen any other physicians?"

"No, she's been quite healthy."

"Where does she go to school?"

"The girls are tutored on my estate."

"So, the girls never get to leave. Is that correct?"

"Of course, we take them on fields trips and special events."

"Mr. Menaphy, what would those girls tell the authorities about their life on your estate?"

"I'm sure they would confirm everything I've said." He didn't sound convincing.

"More specifically, Mr. Menaphy, if Angela testifies this afternoon, what would she tell the court about her life on your estate?"

"Angela? Testify?" The paler Menaphy's face got, the redder the judge's face got.

"Yes, Mr. Menaphy. Angela. It is now clear that she is Rose Kelly's daughter adopted by you under questionable circumstances. We have information that she would testify to reprehensible conduct on your part of the worst possible sort...criminal, abusive conduct, Mr. Menaphy." David's voice rose to full volume. "What would she tell the court?"

The facade cracked. "I, I'm not sure," he stammered. The sweat showed through his hundred-dollar shirt.

The judge leaned forward. "Mr. Greenberg, do you have information on this girl's whereabouts?"

"I believe we do, Your Honor. If our information is correct, she is within the city, in protective custody, and could be here within some forty minutes."

Menaphy wilted like a four-day-old salad. At that moment, Miss Fregossi reappeared with an armload of files and set them on the bench. The judge laid his right hand on top of the stack, eyeing them before speaking.

"Mr. Greenberg, get that young lady to court."

Chapter 34

David turned and motioned for me to approach. "Can you get her here safely?"

"It's my baby, Casey," Rose gasped.

"I know, Rose. I've seen her and she's beautiful. She looks just like you."

David looked intently at me. "And The Death Angel?"

"I'll take Detective Miller with me. We'll protect her."

Rose grabbed my arm, "Joey," she hissed, looking across the room.

He was whispering to Sam. Sam nodded, and then exited the backdoor. Joey smirked at Rose.

I walked briskly to the rear of the courtroom motioning Miller to follow. Sam was nowhere to be seen when we got to the balcony. I filled Miller in as we raced down the stairs. "I've got her hidden in Midtown. I need to call a buddy who's guarding her. But we'll have to watch for Sam as well as the hit man."

"OK, you make the call while I get a cab."

I ran for the phone booth at the corner and called Carl. "Get her ready to go the instant I get there—fifteen minutes maximum."

Miller got a cab and we hopped in. When we reached the hotel, I took the stairs two at a time to our room. Miller told the cab to wait, and stayed in the lobby to make sure we weren't followed. Angela opened the door the instant I knocked.

"Where are we going?" She was dressed and ready. I grabbed her by the elbow and pulled her toward the lobby.

"To see your mother, kid." Her face lit up like Macy's at Christmas. "And to tell your story to the judge about what went on at Menaphy's place."

She jerked like I'd slapped her. "Do I have to?"

"Yeah, kid, but the judge is going to throw the book at him. He's going to prison for a long time. This is your big chance to get even. All you have to do is tell the judge what you told me."

All three of us ran to the cab and piled into the backseat with Angela in the middle. "Back where we came from, cabbie and keep an eye out for a tail."

"You expecting one?"

"Why do you think I asked, buddy?"

It went without a hitch but when we drew up to the courthouse, Sam was casually leaning against one of the front columns.

"See him, Miller?"

"I see."

"Looks like he replaced the pistol, judging from the bulge under his coat."

"Yeah, Stone, but he's got a license. We checked. I can't do a thing about it till he steps out of line."

"Angela, look carefully at that guy. If you ever see him when you're alone, run."

She nodded weakly as we rushed into the lobby, then up the stairs to the courtroom. We had to push through yammering reporters and curiosity seekers. There's no such thing as a secret in the courthouse. You can break wind in the basement and they already know it on the top floor by the time you ride up the elevator.

I turned to Miller. "Sam knows what she looks like now."

"I'm on top of it, Stone. He'll have to go through me."

The bailiff opened the door on our first knock. The judge looked up. Menaphy glared from the witness stand. Joey glared from his seat. Snavely looked back blandly. David gave us a tiny smile. Rose was transfixed.

171

"Bailiff, escort this young lady to my chambers," the judge said smiling at Angela. "Court is in recess until my return." Angela looked at me with fear in her eyes. I patted her on the shoulder and whispered, "Big chance, kid."

The bailiff followed the judge through the door with Angela looking over her shoulder at Rose, who gave her a tentative wave. After the door closed behind them, Rose stared at Menaphy. The hate was so strong, David reached out and held her arm.

Menaphy left the stand and briefly talked to Snavely before leaving the courtroom. After a moment, Detective Brown casually followed. Then Joey stood, stretched, and strolled out the back. All the rats were leaving the sinking ship.

David turned toward us and spoke in a low voice, "The judge has been questioning Menaphy file by file. So far, he's determined that eight of the adoptions are questionable. If Angela tells him what she told you, Casey, he'll void all his adoptions and remove the girls. No doubt he's headed for criminal prosecution. Well done, Mr. Stone!"

I nodded my thanks but wanted to see Menaphy and Joey in custody before I celebrated. And we still had The Death Angel to worry about.

Snavely was alone on his side of the room. "Mr. Greenberg, are you going to push those extraneous charges against Mr. Menaphy?"

"It isn't up to me, Mr. Snavely, but if it were, I'd hang him from the nearest yardarm."

"But you've already won by identifying the girl. Do you really need to ruin a man's whole life?"

"Mr. Snavely, let me be frank. Your client has ruined many lives, using his wealth and position to take advantage of the most vulnerable persons imaginable. Not only would I hang him from the neared yardarm, I'd do so by his privates!"

Snavely looked away in silence. After a moment, he quietly said, "I understand completely."

At that moment, Brown burst into the room. "Menaphy ran! I saw him headed out the door, but couldn't catch up.

I called Captain Butler. He's put out an APB and alerted the task force at The Home and the police on Long Island.

I left Chiquita with my usual warning to be careful and then ran out to the street. I didn't know who I wanted more—Menaphy or Joey. I figured Menaphy's estate was too far for him to run to and headed for The Home. When my cab dropped me off, there were two uniforms guarding the front. Flashing my ID, I asked, "Is Menaphy inside?"

"Don't know. We just got the call to seal this place up...nobody in or out."

"I'm working with Captain Butler, anybody at the rear?"

"Yessir, two other guys."

"I'm going in." They hesitated, but I was already in the front door. I had an idea of the layout from Chiquita's report. The reception room held a frightened secretary and a couple of very pregnant girls huddled in each other's arms in the corner. All three were wide-eyed at my gun.

"Menaphy?" I hissed at the secretary.

Startled, she pointed at the hall and whispered, "Matron's Office. Second door on the left."

I slowed. I had him cornered and I was taking no chances. I wanted him to spend the rest of his life in Attica, getting introduced to the fellows who have daughters on the outside they can't protect.

Gun drawn, I stepped softly toward the office door. I could hear drawers being opened and closed inside. Grasping the knob, I found it was locked.

"Menaphy, there's no escape. Front and back are guarded. Time to give it up."

There was silence. Then the unmistakable click of a gun being cocked. I should have kept my mouth shut!

"No good, Menaphy. You can't get away with it. Besides, we've already copied the records." I lied, but for a good cause.

His voice was high and strained. "You double-crossed me, Stone. All this is your fault." His voice was punctuated by a blast that shattered the doorframe and drove splinters into my left hand. Before I could react, a second blast occurred.

By the time I got to him, he was dead on the floor, his impeccable suit still neat, his countenance strained, his head with a neat hole in the right temple and a mess on the left side. There was no point in checking for a pulse. As I holstered Betsy, I became aware of the screams and sobbing in the reception room and the pounding footsteps of the cops. When they entered the room, they didn't need my explanation.

I walked to the lobby holding my bleeding hand. The secretary took a look and said, "Sit here," giving me her chair. She trotted down the hall and returned with some bandages, disinfectant and tweezers. While she worked on me, Captain Butler charged in the front.

"You OK? Give me the story."

By the time I filled him in from taking Angela into the courtroom to bandaging up my hand, the two pregnant girls had settled to occasional quiet sobs. One of the cops stuck his head in the room to check with the captain.

"Hey," I called to him, "Menaphy put a stack of papers on the desk that probably nail a dozen more felonies on him."

"Get 'em for me," Steve said to one of the cops. "Casey, I've already got a report from Long Island. They've sealed the place, disarmed the security guards, taken the housemothers into custody and are interviewing the girls. Our problem now is finding Joey, Sam, and your Death Angel."

The secretary poured a cupful of disinfectant over my hand, and I jumped and yelped. Steve and the girls laughed. Comic relief wasn't my gig, but it was good to see the girls relax.

"No word on Joey?" I asked through the burn.

"Miller and Brown are both on it, and I've sent an alert all over Manhattan. Nothing yet."

As she finished bandaging my hand, I noticed that the secretary had a pretty almond-shaped face framed by shiny brunette hair. And the rest of her was just as nice. "What's your name, Honey?"

"Sandra."

"Well, Sandra, you can fix me up anytime."

"What's your name, Honey?" she asked with a toss of her head.

Steve interrupted with a big sigh. "It's Casey, Ma'am. Be careful, or he'll be coming around two or three times a day for TLC. I gotta get to work. You keep in close touch, 'Honey'," he said, giving my shoulder a squeeze.

As he walked off, Sandra raised her eyebrows. "Two or three times a day?"

"I hope so, Sandra. Maybe more when I get done with this case." She smiled as she gathered her first aid kit and headed back down the hall.

As soon as I stepped out the front door and saw the ambulance driving up to collect Menaphy's worthless remains, my good mood evaporated. Thoughts of Joey and Sam, and the shadowy Death Angel could darken any sky.

Chapter 35

Fortunately, there was no blood on my suit, and the hand hurt less than I expected. I needed to get back to the courthouse. Chick would be no match for an ambush by Joey and Sam. I was beginning to feel like a yo-yo bounding all over Manhattan.

As I settled into the back of the cab, I propped my elbow on the armrest to keep my hand high, and tried to think. Where would Joey and Sam go? They had been out of town for a few days—maybe enough time for the higher-ups to give Joey a chance to make amends for the shortage in the weekly take. Then again, maybe not. Those guys have long memories when it comes to being cheated. Would he risk going back to his old neighborhood? Probably so, I decided. He grew up there. If he had any friends left, that's where they'd be. Sam had come up with another gun. Joey could too. I needed to talk to Manny and Fu Chen. I told the hack to pull over at the next phone booth and wait for me.

I called Chen's Laundry first. "Uncle Chen? This is Casey Stone. Joey and Sam are back in town. They might show up at your place. If they do, it would be smart to sneak out and call Captain Butler's office. Will you do that?"

"Thank you, Mr. Stone. I will not run away this time. I have two soldiers from my cousin's Tong. They will protect me this time. I told them about Suzie."

I paused. It probably didn't matter what I said. "Please try to call first."

"They will do whatever is necessary, Mr. Stone, but I will try."

"Thank you, Mr. Chen."

I wanted to get Joey myself. Sweet Suzie filled my memory the instant Uncle Chen uttered her name. Black eyes and hair, silky shape, and the scent of jasmine overwhelmed me. I leaned my head against the phone for a moment before I could dial Manny. He answered on the second ring. I gathered myself and gave him the update on everything.

"Manny, I need to find Joey and his goon before they have a chance to get Rose's girl. We'll leave the courthouse with plenty of protection for a while, but ...."

"I know, Casey. I'll put out the word. What about the Chicago hit man?"

"Both of us know what the other looks like, but he knows I'll be at the courthouse, and I don't know where he is. He's got help, so we'll be tailed by an unknown after the hearing. He missed me once inside the courthouse. He won't miss again."

"Any way to get out of there on the sly?"

"I'll have Greenberg ask the judge after the decision. We have to be careful because of the judge's secretary, Miss Fregossi. I'll have to call you back, Manny, I'm moving around too much." I hung up the phone, looked in all directions and got back in the cab.

"You being chased, Mister?"

"It's that obvious, huh? Yeah, I am. I'm a PI on a case to save a girl's life." I showed him my ID.

"Well, I think that cab two cars back is tailing us."

"How many people in it?"

"One, besides the driver. I noticed he stopped for no reason when you got out to make the calls."

"Any way to get behind him between here and the courthouse?"

"I can try. It's one of our cabs. I'll have the dispatcher call him on the radio and put a bug in his ear." He talked into his microphone and in another block, the other cab pulled over to the curb.

"Here we go 'round the mulberry bush," my cabby sang gleefully. When we completed our trip around the block, the other cab was just pulling away from the curb in front of us, still with his passenger who was now motioning frantically.

"Close it up, cabby. In case I get out right quick, here's a twenty to say thanks."

As traffic stopped at a red light, I hopped out, ran and jumped in the cab with gun drawn. It was Sam.

"Where's Joey?" Sam didn't say anything, and I poked the gun in his ribs.

"Just keep going like you were, cabby." He nodded tensely.

"Tell me, Sam."

"Can't tell ya."

"Try harder," I said poking him hard enough with Betsy to cause him to wince. I eased his pistol out and dropped it over the front seat onto the floor. The cabby jumped as it hit. I caught his eye in the mirror and said, "The city will clean your cab if there's a shooting." His eyes went wide.

"Last chance, Sam. I don't have time to play games."

"I dunno. He told me to tail you and get rid of you if I could without creating a stink. Then, I'm supposed to wait in the alley behind the old office till he shows up."

"Who's been collecting the take from the drugs and the girls while you and Joey have been gone?"

"Dunno. Somebody the higher-ups sent."

"Are they still using your office?"

"I guess so."

"What do you know about The Death Angel?"

"Huh?"

"Forget it, Sam. Who shot the CPA?"

"Felix."

"Who shot the girl at my place?"

"Felix."

"Who ran down the judge?"

"Felix."

Alias Baby Girl

"Were you with him each time?"

"Yeah," he said without emotion, looking out the window.

"Who gave the orders, Sam?"

"You know it was Joey."

"Who was giving Joey tips about the case?"

"That broad that works for the judge."

There was silence. I could see the cabby's shocked face in the mirror.

"You know I can't let you go, Sam."

He grunted and the cabby's face went white.

"The only thing that would save your life is giving up Joey. When do you expect to meet him in the alley?"

"Probably nine or ten tonight after it's dark."

"Cabby, head to the Midtown Precinct. Radio your dispatcher and have him call ahead that we're bringing in a suspect to hold for Captain Butler of the Village station."

He reached for the radio in the middle of turning west and ran into a huge pothole. The car jerked and Sam was all over me. One big fist clamped over my gun hand so tight, Betsy wouldn't fire. The other smashed into my ribs, still sore from the glancing bullet two weeks ago and the work over I got last Sunday. As we rolled back and forth fighting for the gun, the cabby slammed to a stop and bailed out. I smashed Sam's still-broken nose and he squealed with pain and loosened his hand on the gun. My first shot went into the door. The second caught his left thigh. He screamed, but didn't quit fighting. The third shot put him out of my misery.

Gasping for breath, I checked myself over. My left hand was bleeding again—I'd forgotten about it—and my ribs were killing me. But there was nothing new. I yelled at the cabby to get back in and take us to the station.

Two down, two to go.

Robert W. Godwin

Chapter 36

The Midtown gendarmes were going to hold me for murder till Steve convinced their Captain otherwise. Even then, they weren't happy about letting me go. I had shown up, dumped a corpse in their lap and was just going to walk out, leaving them a ton of paperwork, a hysterical cabby, and a car that their service department would have to spend hours cleaning up. "Probably never get a payback for it out of the Village," the Duty Sergeant grumped. They didn't even want to let me use their locker room to clean up.

A half hour later, I was back on the street, sore ribs and all. When I got to the Courthouse, Miller was outside watching for me. I grunted with pain as I got out of the cab. We walked together through the lobby and up the stairs.

"Menaphy's shot himself, and I shot Sam. Anything on Joey?"

"You had more fun that we did. We've been on a wild goose chase. Everybody claimed to have seen Joey run off and pointed us in all four directions. Brown is in the courtroom. Everything has been quiet here."

I had just enough time to bring David up to speed when the bailiff opened the door behind the bench and sang out, "All rise." The judge and a smiling Angela entered, followed by a pensive Miss Fregossi.

Angela ran to our table and stopped within a step of Rose who sprang to her feet. The two stood motionless searching each other's faces for a moment before springing into each other's arms sobbing. David produced a handkerchief and

180

tried to quiet them, but the judge said, "Let them be, Mr. Greenberg. This is a reunion sixteen years in the making."

Turning to Snavely, the judge asked, "Where's Mr. Menaphy, sir?"

Snavely looked toward David and answered, "Your Honor, I believe Mr. Greenberg has news for the court."

David wrenched his gaze from the tender scene beside him. "Your Honor, Mr. Menaphy ran from the courthouse during the recess. Our investigator, Mr. Casey Stone, tracked him to The Home and found him going through the files. When confronted, Mr. Menaphy produced a pistol, fired once at Mr. Stone, then shot and killed himself. The police took over from there."

Judge Law sat for a moment drumming his fingers on the stack of files before speaking.

"Gentlemen, I have spent a most informative time with this bright and attractive young woman." He paused, weighing his words. "Based on her testimony, I would have placed Mr. Menaphy under arrest and sent him straight to booking in the custody of the bailiff. But we are spared that due to his demise, the circumstances of which only confirm this young lady's story.

"That leads me to this question, Mr. Snavely. Did Mr. Menaphy have a will?"

"No, Your Honor. He had just revoked his will and we were in the process of preparing a new one. He was, sadly, intestate."

"Maybe not so sadly, Mr. Snavely. He has some thirteen adopted children, including Angela here, who are his legal heirs, entitled to share equally in his estate which apparently runs into many millions. It may be that justice has been done better than we could have imagined. All the girls are minors, and as Mr. Greenberg is already knowledgeable about the matter, I will appoint him and his firm as Trustee for the girls. Setting aside any adoptions later, which I may well do, will not affect their present status as heirs.

"Of course, Angela," he said, smiling warmly at her, "it is clear that you are entitled to the trust your biological father established

"Anything else, gentlemen? No? I presume you will draw the Order, Mr. Greenberg?"

"Indeed I will, Your Honor."

"Then court is dismissed."

As the judge stood to leave, David hurriedly asked, "Sir, may I approach the bench on a totally different matter?"

"Certainly."

They whispered for a moment then the judge beckoned the bailiff to join them. After a few more exchanges, the bailiff nodded assent and the judge left the room in a swirl of white hair and black robe followed by the bailiff and Miss Fregossi.

During the bench conference, Mr. Snavely had packed his briefcase. He stood, shook hands with David and left with a small but friendly nod to Rose and Angela, still tightly holding each other. As he left the room, the noise of the crowd burst through the door, cut off when the bailiff slammed and locked it behind him. He returned and said, "Everyone follow me. Stay close and don't lag behind. Ready?" He took our silence for assent, turned on his heel, and walked briskly through the door behind the bench. David led, followed by Rose, Angela and Chiquita. I was next with Brown and Miller bringing up the rear.

We went through a narrow hallway to an elevator. It barely held the eight of us. As it descended, he said, "This is the way we bring in prisoners from the jail for trial. It leads to a secure area for the paddy wagons to load and unload. When I open the big garage door, you're on your own." He looked down at Angela. "I was rooting for you, Missy. Good luck!" She smiled her thanks through tear-reddened eyes.

The elevator slowed and stopped, and the doors opened onto a stark concrete room large enough for three vehicles with a heavy steel garage door opening to the street. The bailiff selected a key and inserted it into a metal control box activating the door. It clanked open, giving us access to a deserted street behind the courthouse.

The late afternoon sun reflected off the buildings across the street. Miller and Brown scanned the area. Miller spoke.

"The Captain told us to escort you from the courthouse. Where to?"

That was the $64.00 Question.

"I'm OK on my own," said David. "I'm headed back to the office to draw the Order and inform my partners that we'll be handling a major trust for thirteen girls."

"Oh, Mr. Greenberg," cried Rose, throwing her arms around him and kissing his cheek. "How can we ever thank you enough?" David flushed a bit and responded, "Now, now Miss Kelly. I was just doing my job."

She was right, though. "Way to bring down Goliath, David. You wield a pretty impressive sling!"

"Thank you, Mr. Stone," he said, relieved to be diverted from the tearful female.

"People!" Miller pressed. "We gotta get off the street."

David bowed slightly and headed south. I turned to Chick. "Let's put the girls in the room where Angela and I have been staying. You and I will try to get a room next door to keep an eye out until they find Joey. OK?"

"Sure, Boss. Lead the way. I can call my brother to bring some fresh clothes."

Brown used the police call box on the back of the courthouse and five minutes later, two patrol cars appeared. I gave the address and Miller got in the front car and had Rose and Angela lie down in the backseat to avoid being seen. Brown got in the second car and told Chiquita and me to get out of sight as well.

Fifteen minutes later, Rose and Angela were safely locked in the hotel room, and I was arguing with the desk clerk, insisting on an adjoining room. Eying Chiquita, he was complaining about me bringing in girls and turning his hotel into a house of ill repute. Chick was steaming at the implication. Finally, Miller interrupted with his badge and a threat to call in every city inspector he could find if we did not get cooperation. Magically, the adjoining room was ours. After thanks to Miller, I checked on Rose and Angela who barely acknowledged me as their conversation ricocheted over the past sixteen years.

Robert W. Godwin

"OK, ladies, we're next door. I'll order eats. Any requests?" Rose didn't pause, but just gave a little wave over her shoulder.

"Same door procedure, Angela," I called. She nodded without taking her eyes off Rose's face. I laughed and pulled the door shut.

Chapter 37

Chiquita was up the next morning and putting finishing touches on her make-up when I rolled off the sofa with muttered curses caused by my sore ribs.   As I sat and caught my breath, I recalled with grim satisfaction Sam's body being hauled off to the morgue.   Joey waited in vain in the alley last night.   I gave a grunt of satisfaction mixed with pain.   The sore ribs were worth it.   I got an outside phone line and dialed the laundry.

"Chen's Laundry."

"Uncle Chen, it's Casey."

"Ah, Mr. Casey.   How are you?"

"I'm fine, but how are things up there?"

"Some excitement last night."

"What?   Tell me!"

"You remember Joey start to burn my place one night years ago?"

"I do."

"My cousin's two men on guard last night."

"Yes...."

"After dark, they hear something in alley."

"Yes, yes!"

"These soldiers very hard to see at night.   Can move about in secret.   They see man hiding at dumpster.   He just sit.   So they just watch.   Maybe he drunk, you know."

"I know."

"He keep looking at watch and at midnight, get up and try to open my back door with key.   I change lock after Joey and Sam run away. Can't get in. He kick door hard. Hurt foot. Limp away cursing. My men laugh and laugh and tell me this morning."

I laughed too, but it didn't help me get him. I said goodbye and sent Chick out for the deli breakfast—times four—and sat thinking.

Joey didn't like to get his hands dirty, but he'd given the orders that cost three lives. He was a jerk—dangerous, but a jerk. The Death Angel was another matter. I was surprised he'd missed me at the courthouse, even though Menaphy was in the way. Joey was hanging around his old neighborhood. Chicago was still hunting me. He had snitches all over the city, thanks to those flyers that had my picture, addresses, and offered a reward to finger me. Well, I didn't like being on the run, and I didn't like hiding. I had an office and an apartment and wasn't getting to use either one. The more I thought about it, the madder I got.

"Outside line."

When it buzzed, I called Steve. "I can't hide out forever, and I'm fed up with it anyway. I'm going to my office. He already knows where it is and the word will get out to him pronto. I'd rather meet him on my home turf any day."

"Bait, huh?" Gonna use yourself as bait. You're not in shape, Casey. You're beat up with the bad ribs and a bad left hand. You're still showing bruises from the working over Sam and Felix gave you and ...et's face it...you're not the kid you once were."

That hurt. "Stick it in your ear, Captain. I was doing you a favor letting you know, so now you know." I slammed the phone down and my left hand really did hurt.

Chick had returned from the deli and asked, "What's up, Boss?"

I looked at her standing in the doorway and it occurred that you could put Chiquita in bag lady rags, and she'd still turn heads.

"Captain Butler and I are laying a trap for the hit man. I'm headed out in a minute."

Concern clouded her face. "Are you sure? You told me this guy was the best, not likely to fall for tricks."

"We've got a plan," I lied. I was mad, stupid mad maybe, but I was done with being a duck in a shooting gallery. As soon as I freshened up, I took off after giving Chick a peck on the cheek. "Watch the girls."

I nodded to the desk clerk as I walked out the front door, reassured by the weight of Betsy loaded and ready under my coat. No cab today, I strolled to the subway. When I arrived at my station, I took the steps leisurely and sauntered to Jimmy's newsstand where I bought a *Post*. As I paid him, I whispered, "Eyes open, Jimmy. The Chicago hit man is still around." I slowly made my way to the office, reading the paper as I walked. I unlocked my office door, pushing a mound of mail back as I opened it. As I stooped to gather it, the door banged all the way open, knocking me sprawling against Chiquita's desk.

Before I could react, the snarl froze me.

"Don't move, sucker."

I couldn't believe I was so stupid. Getting mad and careless had just bought me my gravestone.

"Joey, you worthless piece of crap. What are you doing down here?" I acted braver than I felt sitting on the floor. Being bait had sure brought in the fish. But the fish had caught the bait instead of the other way around.

"Pull the gun out and scoot it over, shamus." I did so very slowly.

"Now," he said closing the door and sitting on the sofa, "Let's talk a little before you say goodbye."

"I'm not going anywhere, hot shot, this is my office."

"Shut up, or you'll get it right now!" He poked his pistol against my forehead, and I thought I was gone. After a moment, he settled back on the sofa.

"I heard about you taking Sam's body to the station house. What happened?"

"You told him to find me and take care of me. It just turned out the other way."

"He was my best friend, Stone, and you've gotta pay!"

"Best friend?! Who do you think was feeding the scoop to the higher-ups about you skimming the take? Not me. Not Felix. Who?"

A look of uncertainty flitted across his face.

"Who told you that Felix had orders to take you and him out? Huh?!"

More uncertainty.

"How do I know Miss Fregossi was feeding you info?"

I had him.

"Joey, how do I know you and Sam were hiding out in Barnegat this past week?"

The gun dipped as he considered this horrible betrayal that I had made up. I jumped at what might be my last chance. Grabbing the gun with my bandaged left hand I struck his jaw as hard as I could with my right fist. It wasn't hard enough. He was wiry and stronger than he looked. I drove my knee hard for his groin, but he turned just in time and hit me in the temple with a fist that had a ring on his fourth finger. I saw blinding flashes and fell to the floor, but held onto the gun and dragged him with me. He landed on top, scratching madly for my eyes.

I rolled, and he tumbled to the floor. The gun fired and the barrel burned my hand, but the slug hit my framed license on the wall over his head, shattering the glass and knocking it off the hanger. It fell corner-first in a shower of shards into his eyes. As he screamed, I bent his wrist toward his body and the gun fired again. A foot from my ears, it was deafening. I felt him go limp. As sight and hearing returned, I knew it was over.

I released my grasp and rolled to a sitting position, leaning against the desk. Nobody came to check on the ruckus. Maybe I wasn't as popular as I thought. Finally I got up, retrieved Betsy and dialed Steve.

"Captain Butler here."

"Steve, it's Casey. I'm at the office with a dead Joey Catalano."

After the stream of curses stopped, he took a deep breath and asked, "Are you OK?"

"Yeah, but my front office is a mess."

"I'll bet! You were never known for neatness. Casey, do you know what this string of shootings is costing me? I'm answering to my Chief, Midtown personnel, and now

I'll probably get a call from the Commissioner. Damn it, Casey! How 'bout letting the department do its work for a change?" His voice trailed off into another stream of curses.

I let the storm die down a little. "Steve, I'd be in a pickle without you, but remember, it was my office, and it was his gun."

"Yeah, yeah. I'm sending my men over. Try to stay out of trouble for a few days, huh?"

"I'd like that, but it wasn't me that put the flyers all over Manhattan with my picture and a reward on it. Chicago is still out there."

"Geez," he said as he hung up.

Chapter 38

For a few days, all was quiet. I agreed to let Rose return to work and go home with Angel. The girl eagerly accepted the name Rose had always treasured.

Missing me at the courthouse must have been a blow to The Death Angel's reputation. I figured he couldn't go home without dealing with me. I moved back to my apartment and slipped Luther a whole c-note to be especially vigilant. I openly went to and from the office, and traveled my usual routes to Jimmy's newsstand and Pat's bar.

Nothing.

I didn't get careless. I got more and more tense. The storm was coming, but I didn't know when or from what direction.

Rose put Angel in school. She got a disbursement from the trust and outfitted her in new clothes from head to toe. She applied for a two-bedroom apartment in her building and was promised the next available one.

I stayed on perpetual alert and it was ruining my good humor.

Manny hadn't heard anything. Neither had Fu Chen. Steve said police business was back to normal without the trail of bodies behind me. Pat hadn't had any customers but the regulars.

I was in the office late one morning when Rose came by to give me a bonus from the trust with David's approval. It was nice, but the hug that came with it brought back memories of her in a peignoir tied with a ribbon and white-hot passion on her rug.

"When will I get to see you again, my hero?"

"Soon, Baby, soon. But not until I get rid of this guy from Chicago."

"How do you know he's still around?"

"Gut feeling, Rose."

"Well, don't wait too long. Roses don't last forever, you know."

I gave her a lingering kiss and a smack on the bottom as she turned to leave.

"Oh! You naughty boy!" She circled back and earned another one.

I followed her to the door and held it open to watch her walk down the hall. When I closed it gently and turned around, Chiquita's icy glare followed me back to my office.

I shuffled a little mail and decided to celebrate my unexpected wealth with a trip to Pat's to make a deposit against future withdrawals. I blew Chiquita a kiss as I left which didn't thaw her glare at all.

It had become second nature to scan the street for anything unusual. I nodded to a couple of the neighbors and shopkeepers on the way. Everything looked ordinary. It had been several days. Maybe I wrong. Maybe Chicago had been pulled off the job.

In the cool dimness of Pat's Bar and Grill, there were just two retirees in their usual corner, deep in animated conversation. Every day they solved all the city's problems over a couple of Guinnesses. They were as much a part of the furnishings as the tap that drew their ale.

Pat was bent over behind the bar washing glasses. As he nodded hello, I took a stool in front of him and laid a check on the bar.

"That, my friend, should cover my tab for months to come. And I'll have the first beer on it right now."

He dried his hands, picked up the check and made a show of holding up to the light. He then kissed it, laid it in the register and closed the drawer with a satisfied grin. "Coming up, Casey."

As he set the foaming glass down on a coaster in front of me, the phone rang. He stepped to the rear of the bar and answered. With surprise on his face, he turned to me and said, "Casey, it's for you."

"Me?" He nodded and laid the receiver on the bar.

I took another swig of beer and slid off the stool. A couple of steps brought me to the receiver.

"Yeah?"

"He knows you're there." It was him! My mystery informer. "You've got about ten minutes maximum."

Before I could speak, he clicked off. I handed the phone back, heart pounding. Joey getting to drop on me had sapped all the overconfidence out of me. Pat waited with raised eyebrows.

"He says the hit man is on the way. I've got to get out of here, so nobody gets hurt."

"Hold on, Casey, there's just me and them two. They're way in the corner, and I've got this whole bar to hide behind. Besides, you might need some help.

"Thanks, Pat, but I couldn't ask."

"You didn't, Casey! Now can that crap and let's figure out what to do."

He was right, better here in familiar surroundings with a savvy friend, than out on the street. With one eye on the door, I called Steve and told him he had just five minutes to get here.

Would The Death Angel just stroll in the front door? Unlikely, but he didn't build his reputation by being predictable. Then he walked in. He moved easily across the room and took the stool beside me.

Pat played it straight. "What can I get you, sir?"

"Just a bit of privacy, please." The voice was flat, the words ordinary, but his manner was cold and menacing. Pat nodded and busied himself, stacking some glasses near the front of the bar where I knew the sawed off shotgun was within reach.

The Death Angel didn't turn, but watched me in the wall mirror. He clasped his hands in full view on the bar.

Alias Baby Girl

"We haven't met, exactly, but you know why I'm here."
He paused, but I didn't answer.

"I want you to get up and walk out with me. No fuss, no
games, right now."

"Why would I do that, Buster?"

"Because you care for that girl that works for you."

My gut twisted. "She's not involved in this."

"She is a lucky girl, because I hit her from behind and she
never saw me. She's trussed up in that oak chair that faces
your desk. If she wakes up before the gas explodes, she'll
have a headache. If not, she'll roast in peace. On the other
hand, if you and I get there in time, you can take her place.
If not, you'll both die anyway. Clock's ticking."

"OK, OK, we're going."

"First, slip me your .45."

I did, hoping Pat caught it. As we both headed for the door,
I took a chance.

"Gotta get back to the office, Pat, or Chick will be all over
my case." He nodded back nonchalantly.

We slowly walked the two blocks to my office in silence,
my mind racing to find a way to save Chiquita. Pat knew
something was up, and would tell Steve and his cops where
we were headed. I couldn't walk much slower, according
to Chicago's story about the gas. He hadn't frisked me, just
taken Betsy. But what good was my ankle pistol? I'd
never get to it in time. If I failed, Chick died and so did I. I
had a sinking feeling.

As we started up the steps at my building, a man hurried
by us straight to the elevator and pushed the button. He was
pacing impatiently as we approached, and I realized it was
Miller.

The instant the doors opened, he popped in, pushed a
button, and asked, "What do you need?"

"Six," I said, returning his gaze as we entered.

"You got it," he replied, pushing a button.

Exactly on a silent count of six after the doors closed, we
both jumped The Death Angel.

I grabbed him in a bear hug pinning his arms at his side
while Miller drew his service revolver. Chicago brought

193

his forehead down hard into my face. My nose cracked, and I was blinded by the pain, but held tight. He spun me around into Miller who grunted as he was slammed into the railing. I bit Chicago's ear. He jerked, and my mouth filled with blood. I stomped on his foot. He roared and slammed me into the other wall.

The elevator doors opened and a secretary waiting to ride screamed and ran as we fought back and forth. The doors closed, and the elevator rose again.

My grip was beginning to slip, and I was gagging on the blood. Miller hit him in the kidney, and I felt the rush of breath. Then Miller brought the gun down hard on his head with a sharp crack. He sagged, and I fell with him to the floor but he wasn't out.

Chapter 39

We continued to struggle, neither besting the other. I hurt all over from my injuries and was weakening, but held on knowing my life and Chiquita's were at risk. We thrashed about too quickly for Miller to shoot.

Chicago kicked against the corner and levered up on top of me. My ribs were screaming with pain, but Miller got the cuffs on one wrist and jerked hard to reach the other. It broke my grasp. Chicago swung at me twice, hitting my face with the loose end of the cuffs before Miller grabbed it and wrenched his arm behind him and finally got the other arm cuffed.

"Got 'em, Casey!" Miller dragged him off me. I lay bent double, nose bleeding and ribs aching. New cuts and bruises were throbbing, thanks to the flailing handcuffs. I pushed up against the elevator doors just as they opened at my floor and half fell into the hallway.

"Quick, Miller," I gasped. "He says there's a timer in my office and Chiquita is tied up in there."

I rolled over and stumbled to my office. It was locked. As I dug for my keys, Miller dragged Chicago across the hall. Chicago gave a scoffing laugh as I fumbled for my keys. I hit him in the stomach as hard as I could. As Chicago was gagging, Miller yelled at me.

"Hey, none of that, Casey!"

"Miller, that was just the beginning for him."

I finally found the key, unlocked and threw open the door. Chiquita wasn't in the front office and my door was shut. I rushed toward it and grabbed the knob—then froze. I looked back at The Death Angel and caught a grim smile flit across his face. I didn't smell any gas.

"Bring him up here, Miller."

Chicago was bleeding from his left ear and his hands were cuffed behind his back. Miller shoved him toward me. I grabbed him by the throat with one hand and shoved him up against my door.

"Here we go," I said as I turned the handle and pushed the door open with his body. It was halfway open when the blast came. It wasn't gas, it was a trap gun triggered by the swing of the door. The slug slammed him against me as it ripped into his back. We were nose to nose as I watched his face go slack, his eyes roll up and his body go limp. He fell lifeless to the floor.

Chiquita was tied tightly to my oak chair facing my desk. Sobs squeezed through her gag.

"Chick, I'm OK! It got him. Are you OK?"

She nodded. I stepped over Chicago and ripped off her gag and started untying the ropes. She sagged forward as the bounds loosened. I grabbed her shoulders and let the ropes drop. I knelt in front of her. She laid her head on my shoulder, sobbing uncontrollably as I held her.

I was dimly aware of Miller calling Steve on my desk phone, then loosening the rest of the ropes. He left us to keep the curiosity seekers out of the office where they were beginning to gather.

Finally, the sobs eased to occasional tremors. She tried to speak. I held her tight and patted her shoulder. I could see the bloody lump on the back of her head where he'd hit her. At last, she took a shuttering breath.

"Boss, I'm sorry. I'm so sorry. I thought I was dead and taking you with me." Sobs returned. I patted and rocked gently with her.

"No, no, Baby. It was my fault. But it's OK now. He's gone. Everything's OK."

Two days later, I got a note in the mail:
Glad everything worked out.
They won't send anybody else after you.

Alias Baby Girl

Tell Rose I still love her.

.

Epilogue

Within a week, the office was back to normal.

Steve was happy there weren't any new bodies to explain.

Chiquita was happy that her hairdo hid the lump and the small scar where she got hit.

David was happy with the successful lawsuit and new business for the firm.

Carl was happy that his buckshot hit the bad guys and he'd helped rescue Angel.

Pat was happy with the huge deposit I'd made on my tab.

Fu Chen was happy that Joey and Sam were out of his hair forever, and Suzie had been avenged.

Manny was happy that Joey got his just deserts and Rose was safe.

Rose and Angel were happy to be together.

As near as I could tell, everybody was happy except Miss Fregossi, and that made me happy. And the fact that I was taking Maureen to Barnegat for a long weekend. The only thing that bothered me was the mystery of who my informer was. Ah well, there would be plenty of time to find that out when I came back from Barnegat.

Robert W. Godwin, Bob to virtually all who know him, was born in Knoxville, Tennessee five days after Pearl Harbor and nine months and two hours after his parents married. Raised in Knoxville, he graduated from Emory University, Atlanta, Georgia in 1963 and the University of Tennessee Law School in 1965.

Upon being drafted, he served two years in the United States Army in the Staff Judge Advocate's Office, rising to Specialist Fifth Class and receiving the Army Commendation Medal.

Returning to Knoxville, he commenced a civil law practice continues to practice to the present.

An avid runner and triathlete, he has competed in three continents in more than 450 races, including marathons and Half-Ironmans. He and his family have enjoyed bicycle touring both in the USA and Europe. Bob loves travel and savoring new and different cultures and countries.

He grew up hiking the nearby Great Smoky Mountains and is committed to environmental issues as they affect the Park as well as the world at large.

Twice married, with three children, he and his wife are presently raising a teenage grandson. Their home is an 1800's log cabin located in a five acre wood populated with flying squirrels, opossums, raccoons and a variety of other creatures, some of which fancy his style of living and have made his home theirs as well, despite his objections.

He is a longtime columnist for the award-winning journal, *Footnotes,* and has published several articles in local weekly papers. Alias Baby Girl is the first novel in the Casey Stone P.I. series, followed by Bullets, Booze and Babes, and Caper on the Coast.